Charles F. Dole

The Young Citizen

Charles F. Dole

The Young Citizen

ISBN/EAN: 9783337406028

Printed in Europe, USA, Canada, Australia, Japan

Cover: Foto ©Andreas Hilbeck / pixelio.de

More available books at **www.hansebooks.com**

GEORGE WASHINGTON.

BY

CHARLES F. DOLE

AUTHOR OF "THE AMERICAN CITIZEN"

GREAT SEAL OF THE UNITED STATES

BOSTON, U.S.A.

D. C. HEATH & CO., PUBLISHERS

1899

Norwood Press

J. S. Cushing & Co. — Berwick & Smith

Norwood Mass. U.S.A.

THIS LITTLE BOOK

Is Dedicated

TO THE BOYS AND GIRLS OF AMERICA

INTO WHOSE KEEPING

AS CITIZENS AND PATRIOTS

WILL SOON BE GIVEN

THE WELFARE OF OUR NATION

PREFACE.

THIS little book is intended as a reader for the school and home. The author believes that the subjects which it treats ought to be easily interesting to boys and girls. But they must not be presented as task work. It would defeat the purpose of the book to divide it into lessons. The aim of the parent or teacher should be to awaken the natural interest of the children in the things that concern the city and the nation. The only need is that the child shall understand what he reads. Encourage him to ask questions and to talk about the topics treated in the book; also to report and describe whatever he can see with his own eyes or learn for himself about any of these subjects. Develop his sense of pleasure in being a citizen and in looking forward to a citizen's duties. Encourage especially the warm ethical and patriotic feeling, which moves instinctively with the growing consciousness of the child, that right and wrong are involved in politics. Let him see the ideals of cleanliness, public safety, prosperity, and happiness, for the attainment of which governments exist, and he will never easily descend to base and dishonorable conduct. Be sure that he grasps the idea not only that the State is for the sake of the individual, but also that the individual lives for the State; that duties go with rights; that there is no lasting satisfaction except in generous and public-spirited conduct.

The author owes thanks to the Hon. Abram S. Hewitt, Ex-mayor of New York. His earnest and strongly expressed concern in behalf of the multitudes of the children of his own city, whose circumstances cut them off from completing their school course or taking any thorough training in civics, has been a helpful incentive in preparing this book with reference to the need which Mr. Hewitt has so keenly felt. The devoted efforts of Mr. Wilson L. Gill, President of the Patriotic League, in reference to the same practical end, are gratefully recorded.

A series of questions and answers, covering the more important points in this book, and prepared by the author, is published under the same name, *The Young Citizen*, by the Patriotic League, No. 7 East 16th St., New York City. It will be helpful to use this smaller book and to give pupils short exercises, sometimes in answering the questions in their own words, and sometimes in repeating the answers together.

C. F. D.

JAMAICA PLAIN, MASS., *Feb.* 1, 1899.

FIGURE HEAD OF THE NIAGARA.

It is an old custom to have some kind of ornament upon the prow of a ship. How do you like the eagle? Is there something fine or noble about him?

TABLE OF CONTENTS.

ix

CHAPTER XXIII.

CHAPTER XXIV.

CHAPTER XXV.

LIST OF ILLUSTRATIONS.

List of Illustrations.

EQUESTRIAN STATUE OF WASHINGTON.

FOREWORD TO THE CHILDREN
WHO READ THIS BOOK

You have learned by this time something about the vast extent and the enormous natural riches of our country. You have seen on the map how it stretches through thousands of miles, from ocean to ocean. You have followed the courses of its great rivers. You know where its mountain ranges lie. You have read of its vast fields where cotton and corn and wheat grow for the millions of the world. You have seen in what States are mines of gold, silver, and copper, and, what is even more important, of coal and iron. You know some of the cities where the great mills and factories are, and where they build the great ships. Surely no country has such extensive riches or so many happy homes.

Let us see what America has besides all these things which makes it such a good country to live in that men come from every part of the earth to make their homes here. There are other lands which have fertile soil and precious metals, but they are not such happy lands. China, for instance, has vast wealth, but no one wishes to go there to live.

America has that which is better than riches. She has free men who possess the precious inheritance of liberty and just laws. She has the religion of the Golden Rule. Her history is full of splendid stories of patriotism. Her free government fits a brave and free people. Americans are a happy people, but they are not nearly as happy as they ought to be. There are, even in America, too many people who are extremely poor. There are too many children in our land who do not have a fair chance to grow up strong and well and intelligent. Our laws are good, but they ought sometimes to be made better.

This book is written to tell some of the things that you ought to know about our country. They are things that concern every boy and girl in the nation. They ought to make you feel very glad of our country, but, more than that, they should stir you all to do something to help make America a happier country in the twentieth century than it has ever been.

THE PUBLIC GARDEN AND COMMON, BOSTON.

THE BATTERY PARK AND GOVERNOR'S ISLAND, N.Y.

The people have turned what was once the site of an old fort or battery into a pretty garden where one can see all manner of ships and steamers pass by.

THE YOUNG CITIZEN.

CHAPTER I.

THE THINGS THAT BELONG TO US ALL.

A GREAT many things in our town belong to all the people. The schoolhouses with their desks and charts and blackboards, for instance, belong to the people. The fathers and mothers and older brothers of the children, and often men and women who have no children of their own, have paid their money to build the schoolhouses and to furnish them. They have sometimes made the schoolhouses a good deal

better than their own homes.   They have wished to
make the children happy in their schools.

No one can say of the schoolhouse, "It belongs to
me," or "It is mine."   The richest man in the town
cannot say this any more than the poor man.   But

A NEW HAMPSHIRE SCHOOL.

The country schoolhouse of the old times was not always a very
nice place.   It was often hot and stuffy in summer, and cold in
winter, and very shabby altogether.   See what clean and comfortable
schoolhouses the country people are now building.

the poor man as well as the rich man may say, "This
is ours: we own it together."   The children also can
say, "These schoolhouses and all that is in them are
ours."

The schoolhouses are not the only things that all

of us own in common.   Perhaps there are other
buildings which belong to the people.   In a large
town there may be many such buildings; such as the

LAMP-POST AND FIRE-ALARM SIGNAL BOX.

When fire breaks out in any well-managed city, one has no need
to run far without finding an alarm signal box.   Why must it be on
or near a lamp-post?

police-stations, the houses for the fire-engines, the
stables for the horses that draw the city carts, hospitals for the sick, homes for orphan boys and girls,

and a City Hall full of offices.   Perhaps some can
think of other buildings which belong to the people.
The buildings and houses owned by all of us in common are called *public*.   This means that no one can

PLAYING BALL ON BOSTON COMMON.

There is no surer way to keep boys out of mischief than to give
them healthy sports.   The new idea is that all the boys in a city
shall have playgrounds of their own.

ever say, " They are mine," but all can say, " They
are ours."   Whatever is *public* is for every one.

   To whom do the streets belong?   To whom do the

sidewalks and the curbstones and the street-lamps belong?

The street does not belong only to the man who lives on it; the lamp-post does not belong only to the man whose door is lighted by the lamp. The teamsters, the errand-boys, the boys and girls who ride their bicycles to their playground, the people who live on the other side of the town, own the street as much as the men who live on it. Every one who walks out in the evening has a share in all the street-lamps.

Perhaps there is a Common, a Park, or a Public Garden in town; it may be that the land in it is worth a fortune; it may cost the city thousands of dollars every year to keep it in order. But no man is so rich as to say, "It is mine." Every child can say, "It is ours."

There may be a rule that no one shall pick the flowers in the Public Garden, or trample the grass.

But this rule is not to keep us from our rights in the grass and the flowers. The rule is made in order to give us our rights. It is intended to secure the greatest pleasure for the greatest number of people. Is it not better and fairer to give all of us an equal chance to see the flowers, than to let a few pick them and carry them away? The person who takes the flowers from the Public Garden seems to say, "The flowers are mine," which is not the truth.

No one has a right to carry away without permission, and much less to injure, what belongs to us all. Is it not a very good notice which is said to be put up in the public parks of Australia, " *This is your property: therefore do not destroy it*"?

You see now what we mean by *property*. Property is that with which the owner may do as he pleases. Part of the property in town is private; that is, it belongs to some man or woman. A man's house, his ship, his boat, his garden, is private property. He is its owner and he can do what he pleases with it. No one has any right to use it unless the owner gives him permission. But a part of the property in town is public. It belongs to all of us in common. We can do what we please with it — not what any one person pleases, but what we all agree to do or to permit.

CHAPTER II.

IF we travelled across the sea and wandered into a village in Africa, we should be amazed to see how the ignorant people live in the midst of dirt. They have no idea of health or tidiness. They throw bones and ashes, and all sorts of refuse, outside of their huts. The dogs are their only scavengers or health officers. This is the savage way of keeping a town. If the village becomes too bad to live in, huts do not cost much, and the people go to another place and build a new village.

Not all the bad towns, however, are among savages. We have heard of towns nearer than Asia or Africa where we would not choose to live. The streets are filthy and unwholesome; all sorts of rubbish are thrown into them; a lady would have to pick her way along the dirty sidewalks with great care amid orange peels and banana skins.

What is it that makes such a city so disagreeable? The trouble is, that the people are careless; they have no good rules about keeping their streets clean; or if they have rules, they break them, and scatter

9

papers and various kinds of unsightly things in their streets.

There are parts of towns, even in America, where a citizen would be greatly ashamed to take a visitor. "What a dirty and tumble-down place this is!" the visitor would say. Or he would say, "How noisy

STREET CLEANER.

See what a clean way is here used for handling the dirt of the streets. The street-cleaning men hardly need to soil their fingers.

and disorderly the people are!" Perhaps the stranger would observe pieces of glass in the street, and looking up would see that the street-lamp had been broken. His friend would explain to him, "The boys down here break the city lamps."

Perhaps the visitor would go into one of the schoolhouses. Suppose he should find the desks cut and the blackboards scratched and spoiled, and writing on the walls of the buildings. Suppose he should see boys walking or standing about with cigarettes in their mouths, or throwing stones at the lamp-posts. He would say, "I do not wish my children to come here to live."

How does a town get a bad name? It gets a bad name from the ill manners of its people, from the ugly look of its streets, sidewalks, and schoolhouses, and from the behavior of noisy and disorderly persons.

How then can children help to give their town or their city a good name? What can they do to make strangers and visitors enjoy coming and staying in the place? What will bring the right kind of people to live in the town? What can children do to make the town a fine home for themselves and their friends?

The first thing they can do is to take good care of their own schoolhouses. If they do this they will never mar the walls, or cut and injure the desks, or make them unsightly. They will keep their desks in order; they will not mark or soil their schoolbooks.

They will see to it that their own sidewalks and the sidewalks about their schoolhouse are not littered with papers and rubbish. They will talk and laugh in the streets as much as they like, but they will not make disagreeable noises. They will be orderly on

their way to and from school, so that no one will ever
have to move away from the neighborhood of the
schoolhouse on account of the boys.

They will be respectful to older people and especially to strangers. They will be respectful to the
people who wear plain clothes, as well as to those
who wear the latest fashions; to those who walk as
well as to those who come in carriages. They will
be kind to all, and doubly kind if any one is lame, or
sick, or unfortunate.

If they are good Americans, they will never be less
kind to any one on account of the color of his skin,
whether it is brown, or yellow, or black, or white.
The children who wish their town to have a good
name will treat others as they themselves would wish
to be treated if they ever went to live in a strange
place, where no one knew them; or if all the other
people in town were Russians or Chinamen, and they
were the only Americans.

The children who wish to make a good name for
their town will take good care of themselves and of
their clothes. They will choose to be tidy and clean,
with clean faces and clean shoes, with happy and
good-natured faces also. They will like clean words,
such as become the young citizens of a clean and
noble city.

They will set the fashion in their school against all
filthy and profane language. Will they not set the
fashion also against cigarettes and tobacco? Why
should boys who want to grow strong and be well,

THE GRAND CAÑON OF THE YELLOWSTONE.

This beautiful scenery belongs to the people of the United States to enjoy forever. The big river leaps here three hundred feet into a deep channel or cañon cut by the water in the rock. The steep sides are many hundred feet in height.

enfeeble themselves with tobacco? Surely all the doctors agree that as long as boys are growing, tobacco enfeebles them. When you see boys smoking you may know that they are not being well brought up; when they are men they will lack manly vigor.

TENNIS COURTS, FRANKLIN PARK, BOSTON.

Here is a chance for the girls and women, as well as for the men, to have capital exercise. There are also golf-links which the city provides in the same park.

Once more, the children can make up their minds pretty early what kind of a city they intend to live in. They can decide that when they are old enough to vote, they will so vote as to make their city the cleanest and most beautiful place in which to live. They

will vote to have plenty of good water and bath-
houses. They will vote to keep the streets well
paved and brightly lighted. They will vote to get
rid of the houses where disease always lurks, and to
let the light into the dark, damp places where it is
not now safe for little children to live. They will
vote for true and honest men, who believe in the
children and in the schools, and in making the city a
city of real homes ; that is, a city of God.

CHAPTER III.

WHAT SCHOOLS AND TEACHERS ARE FOR.

EVERYWHERE throughout the United States one sees schoolhouses. In many cities they are the finest and costliest buildings. The school property of our country is probably worth more than all the lands and farms and shops and palaces of many an ancient kingdom. All of the gold and silver that comes from all the mines in the land is hardly worth so much as the people spend every year in paying their teachers, and in making the schools comfortable for the children. Many parents also, who are very poor, and who badly need the help of their boys and girls in earning money, go without their help in order to send them to school. In some States the laws require parents to send their children to school a certain number of weeks every year.

What is the use of going to school? Why should the people pay such great sums of money for the sake of having good schools? Why would it not be as well to let the boys and girls go to school or not as they choose? How many children, we wonder, would like to be quite free of the duty of going to school?

Let us try to think what would happen if all the schools were closed, and the millions of school children

STEELE HIGH SCHOOL, DAYTON, OHIO.

The best of the newer schoolhouses are among the most costly and spacious buildings in America. Their architects have sought to make them beautiful works of art. Their builders have used the most solid material so that they may last for centuries.

were sent into the streets or the fields, or were put to work.   We do not need to suppose this.   We need only to learn about· Africa or Turkey, or any barbarous country.   We need only to read about England as it was at the beginning of this century.   The

LONGFELLOW.

Think how many different kinds of men are needed to do the work of the world!   The poets are quite as necessary as the engineers and the bridge-builders.   Thousands of American boys and girls have been stirred to be better citizens by reading Longfellow's " The Building of the Ship."

rich could go to school, but the children of the poor toiled in factories or in mines, and grew up in ignorance.   Which are the best countries in the world to live in ?   They are those, like America, where the people take good care of their schools. Which are the best cities and towns in America? They are the places where the schools are the best.

STATUE OF PETER COOPER.

When a man has done brave or generous service for the people, they like to set up a statue of him in bronze or stone in some public place to remind men that all ought likewise to be brave and generous. Peter Cooper, who had been a poor boy, left a great fortune for the benefit of the people of New York City.

But why would it not be as well to let those children go to school who choose, and allow the others to play or to work? Suppose we tried this plan; and suppose that in the course of a few years, when the children grew up, we had two classes of people in the town, — the educated and the ignorant! You see, we do not want two different classes in America, one class superior to the other. We want all the people as well educated as possible.

What will education do for us? some one asks; for it is hard work to sit still, to study, to work out questions in arithmetic, to write and to draw well.

Education is power.   It is power to earn money.
What if a man does not know how to read?   He will
find a hundred doors to employment shut in his face.
The more a boy knows, the more he is wanted.   Can

TENNYSON.

Here is a man whose verses are read wherever the English
language is spoken.   He has taught men to be noble and brave and
pure, and to love freedom.   Englishmen and Americans, Canadians
and Australians, become like one people whenever they read the
great poets.

a boy write well and add up columns of figures without making a mistake?   That boy, if he is honest, is
wanted at once.   There are not enough boys of this

sort to fill the places. Can a girl draw well? Can she make designs? Is she quick to catch an idea? That girl will have better wages, the more skilful she becomes. Yes! Knowledge is a kind of power. You store it up, as you store up electricity in a battery. But it is better than electricity, for power of that kind may be used up ; but the more you use your knowledge, the greater the store becomes.

Knowledge is also the power to enjoy. To be able to read is to enjoy all sorts of things which the ignorant cannot touch or see. To read is to have friends in every library and every good newspaper or magazine. Longfellow and Tennyson, Washington and Franklin and King Alfred, become our friends, as soon as we are able to read.

The country wants something more of its boys and girls than to know how to earn a living and to enjoy themselves. It wants brave, intelligent, and noble citizens. Here is the great reason why every one must be sent to school.

Suppose our people were as ignorant as the people are in Mexico and Brazil and Cuba. They could not even read the head-lines in the newspapers. They could not read the names on the ballots on election day. Or, suppose they did not know the difference between one party and the other; for example, between Republicans and Democrats; suppose they did not know for what they were voting. The truth is, no one's life or property is safe till the people know enough to vote for good men and just laws.

Knowledge is power to see what is good for the country or for the city. The ignorant man does not see what use there is in the schools. He does not see why he should pay money for them. It may be that he does not see why he should be compelled to keep the laws.

METROPOLITAN MUSEUM OF ART, NEW YORK.

This large and beautiful building is used for keeping and exhibiting paintings and other works of art. Many of these precious things belong to the city. Sometimes wealthy friends of the people lend their own pictures so as to give every one a chance to enjoy them.

We send our children to school in order that they may learn what the best things are for their city and for America. The more they know, the more they will want the best for their city, — good roads, fine water, safety from fire and mischief, honest and truthful officers. The more they know, the better they will see what is good, not for the North alone, or the West, or for New York, or Iowa, but for all the people of America.

We want more than knowledge. We want friendliness. The schools teach us not to be mean, stingy, and selfish, but just the opposite. All the children are comrades.

We do not ask in our American schools who a boy's father is, or who a girl's grandmother was. We all meet on one level as fellow-learners. We want what is good, not for one, but for all. We learn to become friends of one another. We are friends also of all the school children. Throughout the United States they are like us. They learn the same lessons, they salute the same flag; they are all learning, as we are, to become true-hearted Americans.

There was a queer, false notion once, that teachers and pupils were against each other. The pupils tried to make trouble for the teachers, and the teachers whipped the pupils, and "broke their wills." We do not believe any longer in America that teachers and pupils are against each other. The teacher is not paid to punish children, but to help them. The teachers and the children are friends.

We do not wish to break the will of an American boy or girl. We wish a boy or girl to have a very strong will. We only ask that it shall be a *good* will, — the will to help, the will to make the school a splendid success, the will to learn ; a friendly will toward all, a will to be honorable and high-minded.

CHAPTER IV.

WHO have the right to be called true American citizens? Perhaps some one will say: "I have the best right to be called an American. My family is one of the oldest in the country. My ancestors came over here when there were only a few Indians on these shores. One of my forefathers came in the famous little ship *Mayflower*. One of my great-great-grandfathers came from Holland with the Dutch settlers, who founded the State of New York. Some of the men of my family fought with Washington in the war for freedom. I have the right to belong to the Sons (or the Daughters) of the American Revolution."

All this is very interesting, but what do you think the Indian chief Massasoit, who helped eat the first Thanksgiving dinner in America, would say to this fine speech? We can guess, if Massasoit could speak, what he would answer back to the boy or girl who wants to be thought a better American citizen than the other children: "Your father," the big Indian might say, "came here to my land a stranger and very poor. I could have gathered my warriors and

25

driven him and his friends into the sea.   But I pitied
them and helped them.   My fathers had been in this
land for countless years.   We were the first and true

CELEBRATION IN NEW YORK OF THE ADOPTION OF THE
CONSTITUTION.

It was not enough for soldiers to fight for American liberty.
After the war was over the wisest men in the country had to come
together and make a plan of government.   Not till then could the
country be happy.

Americans.   We owned the corn-fields; we let the
white men share the land with us.   What right have
you boys and girls, whose forefathers were strangers

and emigrants, to set yourselves up as better Americans than others?"

ALEXANDER HAMILTON.

We may begin to hear other voices speak along with the old Indian chief. There was a famous

American named Alexander Hamilton.   He lived in
New York.   He was a great friend of Washington,
and was one of his bravest officers.   He was one of
the ablest and brightest men of his time, and he

helped to estab-
lish our Republic.
But he was born
in one of the West
India Islands.
His father was a
Scotchman and
his mother was
French. He came
from home to a
school in New
Jersey when he
was only a boy.

Let us hear what
he would say to the
boys and girls who
think that they are
better Americans
because their fam-
ilies have been
longer in the
country.

JOHN BOYLE O'REILLY.

Mr. O'Reilly was an American citizen,
"by adoption," as we say. He was born
in Ireland and risked his life for what he
thought his duty to the Irish people. When
he came to America he gave his whole
heart for the good of the American people.

"Do you mean to tell us," Hamilton would say,
"that your people loved America more, or did her
more stalwart service, than I did? What stories I
could tell you children about the brave deeds of my

IMMIGRANTS.

The immigrants come to our shores in great ship-loads. Whole families, parents, grandparents, and little children, often come together. Sometimes they are so poor as to bring hardly anything besides their clothing. From what distant land do they not come with high hopes of America!

friends, who, like me, were immigrants to America. Was there ever a better American than the great-hearted German Baron Kalb, who came over here ready to die, fighting for liberty?"

And now others speak to us: "We came over strangers and immigrants, like your ancestors, from Ireland, England, Norway, and many another home in the old countries. You needed us, and we helped you in the great Civil War. Thousands of us fought for America. You needed us in your mines and on your railroads. Where do you find any men and women who love the flag more than we do? Do you think you can find any better Americans than John Boyle O'Reilly or Carl Schurz?"

The truth is, we cannot make any division in America because some families have been here longer than others. The Indians would certainly be the best Americans, if we valued our citizens for the length of time their families had lived in this country.

Neither can we call some boys and girls better Americans than others, for what their forefathers did. Suppose there was a great-grandson of Washington in our school, and suppose he was tardy every few days, and did not learn his lessons, and disobeyed the rules, and made the teachers trouble, and was uncivil to strangers in the street; and suppose that there was by his side at school a little Italian or Russian boy, who had just come over here, but who was prompt and faithful and obedient and good-tempered; this young Washington would not be half so good an American as the other boy.

Whom, then, shall we call the best American citizen? Who is the best kind of pupil to have in the school? We do not ask who gets the best marks, or learns the lessons quickest, or makes the fewest mistakes. We mean the best all-round boy or girl, good in school and good in games too, whom the teacher likes, but whom the children like also, friendly and helpful at home as well as at school, kind and brave, honest and generous.

BUNKER HILL MONUMENT.

How many of the pupils can tell the story of Bunker Hill? The great monument is 224 feet high. There is a stone staircase to the top of it, where one can have a grand view over the ocean and all about Boston.

Show us boys and girls like this, and we will tell you who will make the very best American citizens. We do not care in what land across the ocean their parents were born, or what language they can speak besides our common English tongue. We do not care whether they are rich or poor.

Teach them about our history; it belongs to all of us in common. Tell them the stories of our heroes. Show them what kind of a country we are trying to make of America — the land of happy homes, the land of beautiful cities, the land of freedom and justice. Give us plenty of true-hearted boys and girls, thousands and millions of them, and we will have in a few years the very best American citizens.

CHAPTER V

WHO PATRIOTS ARE.

WHO are the patriots in America? No doubt many would answer at once, "The patriots are the men who fight for their country; the men who stood with Warren on Bunker Hill, and with Sumter and Marion and Morgan in the Carolinas; the men who made Cornwallis surrender at Yorktown; the sailors who fought alongside of Paul Jones; the sailors on the good ship *Constitution;* the soldiers who followed Grant to Richmond; the men in Farragut's fleet.

"Yes," some would say, "the men who rode with Custer on the plains of the far West, Dewey and his men at Manila, Roosevelt and Hobson at Santiago, —all these were patriots. They were the same kind of patriots as the famous Spartans, who died ages ago at the pass of Thermopylæ [1] over in Greece, of whom the orators and poets have spoken and sung ever since."

There is something wrong in thinking that patriots must be soldiers and sailors. What shall we say of

---

[1] The Greek word Thermopylæ means the Warm Springs.

34

the women who do not fight? What shall we call
Martha Washington, who had to stay at home while

U. S. GRANT.

her husband was at Valley Forge? What shall we
call the thousands of women who sent their brothers

and sons to help Washington and Grant? Were not
these women as good patriots as their husbands and
brothers? Indeed the women often had the hardest
time. They had to carry on the farms, while the
men were away; they suffered from anxiety and

BENJAMIN FRANKLIN.

Born a poor boy, he became famous in Europe as well as America.
He was a pioneer in the history of newspapers, of the post-office, of
almanacs for the people, and of electrical science.

loneliness. For many a brave woman it would have
been easier to die herself, than to send her boy away
to die with wounds or with fever. We must surely
call all brave women patriots who love their country

well enough to let their husbands and sons go to war
for the sake of the flag.

We must not forget a multitude of men who, even
in the War of the Revolution and in the great Civil
War, were never soldiers or sailors, and yet were
patriots. There was Benjamin Franklin, for instance.
He did not fight, but
who loved America
better than he? If
it had not been for
his services at the
French king's court, no
one knows how many
weary years the war of
Independence might
have lasted.

There was Samuel
Adams, — who ever
heard of his fighting
a battle? But he was
as brave and sturdy a
patriot as any soldier
could be. There was

ROBERT MORRIS.

Morris was a Philadelphia man.
He was rich, and willingly risked his
fortune to help raise money to pay
Washington's soldiers.

Washington's friend, Robert Morris of Philadelphia,
who helped get money to pay the soldiers.

Where, indeed, in the time of war would all the
wheat and beef come from to feed the army, and the
clothing to keep the men warm, if there were no
patriots hard at work on their farms and in their
shops? Who shall say that the men at home do

not love their country as well as the men who fight in the field? Why is it not good patriotism to work for the country and pay taxes cheerfully for the needs of the government?

STATUE OF COLONEL PRESCOTT.

Prescott was the leader who fortified the heights at Bunker Hill and commanded the Americans there. His statue stands where he fought.

We must not forget another set of good patriots in the times of Bunker Hill and Valley Forge. They were the patriot children who were not yet old enough to fight for their country, but who were, nevertheless, perfectly willing to do so if they had been wanted. These patriot boys and girls, all the way from Portland to Savannah, rushed out, you may be sure, whenever a horseman came riding into the village bearing news of the war. They helped their mothers and sisters while their fathers were away. They were full of gladness, too, when at last the long war was over, and by and by they told to their children the stories that their fathers had told to them, — about the troublous and dreadful years of the war, and the heavy cost that had purchased our liberties.

Were there no patriot boys and girls also on the side that was beaten in the Revolution? Were none of the men patriots who believed it their duty to go into exile rather than to fight against their own mother country? Was not Governor Hutchinson in Massachusetts a patriot as well as John Adams and Hancock? Suppose a man is mistaken, or is on the losing side, cannot he still be a patriot, if he truly loves his country?

JOHN ADAMS.

We are on the right track now to find out who patriots are. It was quite a mistake to suppose that patriots must be fighters, or

John Adams was one of the Massachusetts patriots and the second President of the United States. He was the man who, when British soldiers were tried in Boston for firing upon the people, held it to be his duty to defend them and to give them a fair trial.

that they must live in a time of war. Through all the history of our country, from the Declaration of Independence to the present year, we have lived most of the time without war. Most of the time we have had only a few soldiers, and we have had very little for them to do. The fact is, we are not a fighting people. Why should any one want to go to war, and burn towns and kill men? That is what barbarous people do, but we in America mean to live like civilized men. We do not believe in fighting, unless duty compels us to fight. Who knows but that they are right who say that there is *always* a nobler way than to fight?

THOMAS JEFFERSON.

Jefferson was one of the great men of Virginia. Few men ever did more for the country or loved its liberties better than this hero of peace. He was the third of our Presidents.

Do you think now that the millions of Americans who have lived in the times when there was no war, were not just as good patriots as ever lived or fought? To be a patriot is to love one's country; it is to be ready and willing, if need comes, to die for the country, as a good seaman would die to save his ship and his crew. We think that the seaman should be willing to die, but we do not wish him to die. We wish him to be skilful

ABRAHAM LINCOLN.

See what a kind, rugged, homely face this is. No one was ever
a better friend of the people. Find what you can about his boyhood.

enough to keep clear of the dangerous ledges, and to live, and to bring his ship safely into port, voyage after voyage. So we do not wish the good citizens to die for their country, but to be just and fair and wise, and to treat the people of other nations as their friends, and so to live nobly for their country. We think that Washington and Grant were as true patriots when the country was at peace as when it was at war.

DANIEL WEBSTER.

This is the man who said, "Liberty and Union, now and forever, one and inseparable."

Yes! To love our country, to work so as to make it strong and rich, to support its government, to obey its laws, to pay fair taxes into its treasury, to treat our fellow-citizens as we like to be treated ourselves, — this is to be good American patriots.

"Ah!" some one may say, "did not the men and women have to be braver in the war times than in time of peace?" Let us stamp that as false. What a terrible thing it would be to be brave, if bravery requires of us to hurt and kill! Is it not brave to try to save life? Thousands of brave men are risking their lives every day to help men and to save us all from harm. Brave doctors and nurses go where deadly disease is, and are not afraid to help save the sick. Brave students are trying perilous experiments, so as to find out better knowledge for us all. Brave engineers on thousands of locomotives are not afraid of sudden death if they can save their passengers from harmful accidents. Brave sailors are always facing the sea and the storm. Brave firemen stand ready to die to bring little children safely out of burning buildings.

THE MINUTE-MAN, CONCORD, MASS.

The Minute-men were the citizen-soldiers, whom the British found in 1775 at Lexington and Concord. They were called minute-men because they were ready to fight at a moment's call to defend their country.

Brave boys every summer risk their lives to save their comrades from drowning. Brave fellows hold in check maddened horses and prevent them from running away with women and children. Brave women risk their own lives daily for the sake of others.

Wherever we see a brave man, or woman, or child, there we look for a patriot. Whoever is brave to help others will be brave also for the sake of his country. Never forget it : it is better to be brave to help men than it is to be brave to harm them.

CHAPTER VI.

DANGEROUS PEOPLE.

OUR country is very large; it has many millions of people; it contains great cities; it is rich in its fertile fields, in its forests and mines, in its great factories, its workshops, its railroads, and its ships. But we must not think because our country is strong and rich that it is safe from dangers. Let us see what the dangers are against which America asks its sons and daughters to help make it safe.

In the first place, there are great multitudes of ignorant people in our country. Many of them are so ignorant that they cannot even read or write their own names. Some of these very ignorant men and women live in towns and cities and pass schoolhouses every day as they go to their work. Others live on farms scattered all over the land; sometimes they are miles away from any school; their children grow up as ignorant as the parents are. If we could gather together all these people who cannot read, and have them march ten abreast, they would make a procession hundreds of miles in length.

We must not blame these ignorant fellow-citizens of ours for not having gone to school. Most of

them never had a fair chance to learn. Some of
them were born in slavery, or their parents had been

A GROUP OF LOAFERS.

Why are these men dangerous to the city? Not surely because
they are poor, or because they are ill dressed, but because they are
idle and lazy and mean. Is there one of them who looks as if he
had ever earned an honest living?

slaves. Some of them were born in foreign lands,
where there were no schools except for the rich.

Some of them had to go to work when they were little and were never afterward able to leave off work to go to school. In large parts of our own country, the schools are opened for only one short term each year, and the children are apt to forget what they have learned before they have the chance to go to school again.

Of course there are some people who are ignorant because they did not want to go to school, or because they played truant. But on the whole we must pity the ignorant people rather than blame them. Most of us would have been ignorant too, if we had been brought up far away from any good schools, or in homes where no one ever taught us to read.

It is extremely dangerous to America to have whole armies of ignorant people. The danger is not because ignorant people wish to do wrong. They may earnestly wish to do right. The danger is that they cannot easily tell what is right, or what is best for the city and the country. They hear one side of a question, but they cannot read, so as to know about the other side and make up their minds fairly.

The ignorant have to act and sometimes to vote, without knowing what their actions or their votes will do. Bad or selfish men lead them astray, and because of their ignorance they never find out that they are being used by selfish men for bad purposes. The ignorant are more easily excited than the intelligent. They lose their heads, and then they do things which work mischief; perhaps they destroy property, or even take life. They may be very sorry afterward, but it is too late to repair the damage. Many a time has war come about on account of the sudden passions of the ignorant.

Moreover, it is hard to find work enough for a great mass of ignorant people to do. They cannot do skilful or nice work, and there is not enough rude work like digging to keep them all busy. This want of work makes them poor, and keeps them poor, and the poorer they are, the harder it is for them to give their children any help toward an education.

The ignorant people are not our enemies; we all

THE PILLORY.

See what cruel and shameful punishments our forefathers used to inflict. Do you suppose it ever made people better to treat them in this way?

wish to help and befriend them. But ignorance is an enemy of our country. We must unite to drive it out of our land. We must all be torch-bearers and

flood the darkness with light.   We cannot afford to
have any of our people left poor and miserable.

Ignorance is not our only enemy.   There are
violent and hurtful people whom nobody wants for
neighbors.   There are tricky and dishonest people,
of whom we have to beware lest they rob and cheat
us.   There are drunken
people who make life
very wretched for every
one who has to live with
them.   There are idle
and lazy people who
sponge on their. friends
and relatives, and man-
age to get a living with-
out working for it.

WHIPPING AT THE CART TAIL.

Here is another of the cruel and
useless punishments of the old
times. The worst of it was that
sometimes good men were treated
in this way.

"Yes," you say, "these
people are dangerous
for their neighbors, and
even for their own fami-
lies, but how are they
dangerous to America?"
Why! These lazy, drink-
ing, passionate, or tricky people are a part of America.
They are like sores on a man's body. If he has even
a few sores, he is uncomfortable, but if he has many,
they sap his strength, and after a while if they increase,
they kill him.

These dangerous people help make our laws and
choose our officers to govern us.   But how can dis-

honest men make honest laws? What if the idle and the tricky men get into the offices? Then they will misuse and waste the money of all the people. When the bad men get the places of honor and trust, it is as if sores fastened themselves to the man's heart and lungs. So it kills a nation if the people let the passionate, the selfish, and the careless take charge of the great and costly machinery of the government.

We are not saying that the idle and the dishonest people mean to do all this harm to their country. Some of them are too ignorant to know how mean it is to get a living out of other people. They have never been told that ugliness, quarrelsomeness, drunkenness, cheating, and sponging are like diseases. They have never been told that the mean, dishonest, and idle are a great load that the nation has to carry on its shoulders.

Perhaps we ought to pity these hurtful people just as we pity the ignorant. But whether we blame them or pity them, they are no less dangerous to America. As we love our country and wish to see it strong and great, we must contrive to kill out the cheating and laziness and hard drinking and ugly manners that disgrace every large American town, and threaten to drag our nation down to the level of a barbarous country.

CHAPTER VII.

EVERY one has heard the story of poor Benedict Arnold. He began by being a patriot. It was a great pity that he did not die in the battle of Saratoga, which he had helped so gallantly to win. But he fell into a great temptation, and betrayed the cause of his country. This was *treason*, and his name comes first in our minds when we think of a great traitor.

It is not only in war that a man may be as really a traitor to his country as Benedict Arnold was. A man may commit treason against his country in time of peace. See how this may be.

Treason is to go over to the side of the enemy. But what are the constant enemies of America? Our enemies are not across the ocean; they are here with us. We have already found out what they are. They are injustice, dishonesty, lying, lawlessness, greed, and selfishness. These enemies live in the hearts of men and women. Suppose all the millions of our American people should fight these enemies, and drive them out; or, what is the same thing, suppose our people should go over to the side of the true men, the faithful, the generous, that is, to the side of the patriots. Then no harm could come to our country. A nation of honest, just,

BENEDICT ARNOLD.

We ought to be very sorry for Arnold. He began by being a brave and loyal patriot. Washington loved and trusted him. What a shame that such a man should have become vain and conceited, and at last false to his friends and his country!

true-hearted, and friendly people is invincible. No one ever wishes to do them harm.

What will happen, if even a part of the people give themselves up to their enemies, and lie and steal and wrong one another? A hundred years ago, when the nation was still young, there was an able man who did this sort of thing. His name was Aaron Burr. He was at one time the Vice-President of the United States. He had a fine education. He was the grandson of one of the best men who had ever lived in Massachusetts.

No one ever had a more splendid chance to serve the country and leave an honored name. But he was utterly selfish. He wanted more than was right. This is what the thief wants. He had ambitions for himself rather than for the welfare of our country. His life became bad and dishonorable. He quarrelled with Hamilton and killed him in a duel. He made wild, if not quite treasonable, schemes, all of which came to ruin. He lived to a lonely old age. It would have been better for himself and his country if he had died young. For his selfish ambition made him a traitor and enemy to his country.

No outside enemy can be so dangerous in fighting against us as selfish and dishonest citizens are. If there ever should be at one time many such men as Burr, we could not have a government or be a nation.

What made Aaron Burr so bad a traitor? Why was he more dangerous than a great crowd of merely ignorant men? It was because he knew better than to do wrong. He had been educated to do right, and he did wrong with his eyes open.

The most dangerous men for America are the traitors like Burr. They are men who know better than to do wrong. They have had good homes, good friends, good education, good fortune, and, in spite of all these things, have deserted their post and gone over to the enemy. Their country says to them, " We depend on such men as you to stand for the laws, to be faithful to your duties as citizens, to choose and support good officers, to lift the standards of good government, to do your fair share, and a little more than your share, to make America the noblest land in the world."

AARON BURR.

You would think that this might be the picture of an old-fashioned gentleman? Who would have guessed that he was a dangerous man? The truth is, the more a man knows, the more harm he does in case he is mean or selfish.

That is what the country says to its educated men and women. What shall we think of people who are so mean as not to heed this call? Let us not be afraid to class them with Arnold and Burr. They may not be able to do as much mischief as these great mischief-makers did. They may not actually kill

better men than themselves.   But such men as these
are all the time trying in one way or another to do
what Burr tried to do ; namely, to use the government
of the city or of the nation for themselves, so that
they may make money, or get the offices.   Whereas
patriots conduct the government for the good of all
the people.

All that we have said about traitors and patriots
comes straight home to the school children.   We
might forgive some poor Armenian, who came over
here too ignorant to know anything of our American
history, or some African whose forefathers had been
slaves, if he voted for mean men and unjust acts.
We could even forgive him if he thought that the
government was intended to give an idle man a
living.

But we could not well forgive one of our own
children, trained in our public schools, if he should
go over to the enemy.   Our schools teach them that
the government is for the sake of us all, like the
reservoir of water that fills all the great mains of
the city and supplies every faucet in every house.
What an outrage it would be if some one should
waste or pollute the water that belongs to us all!

There are young men in our cities who were born
of our most honorable families.   Their parents have
often been very generous and public-spirited.   They
have had great wealth ; they have given their boys
every advantage ; they have sent them to the great
universities.   These boys have learned what America

asks of her sons. You will not envy these boys for a moment when you are told that they have been living the lives of traitors to their country. They are often as idle as any tramp on the streets. They hang around their fine club-houses and do nothing but smoke and drink and talk. They have never tried to do anything for the public good; they have drawn the water freely from the great reservoir, and they are not willing to pay their share for it, or to help keep the great mains in repair.

What a chance these boys would have if they would stop acting the part of traitors! They might use their money to give better education for the people. They might use some of their time for the public service. They might join hands and redeem their city from misrule and waste. They might give America the noblest and purest government that the world ever saw. Let us be glad that some of the rich young men are trying to do this very thing!

CHAPTER VIII.

THE time was, when the whole world was divided into warring cities and kingdoms. If a man from the Hebrew land went up to Samaria or over to Damascus, he took his life in his hand. So if an Egyptian went over the sea to the Island of Cyprus or to Greece, he travelled at great risk. The little country of Greece was once full of cities unfriendly to each other. An Athenian would have found enemies in Sparta or Thebes. Even a hundred years ago the map of Europe was cut up into a great many little states, each with its separate laws and governments. There was not one great Germany, but many little German states. There was not one Italy till quite lately.

We in America also began with thirteen different colonies. The people of Massachusetts were jealous of New York and Virginia. The people of Rhode Island and Delaware were afraid that the greater colonies would do them wrong. It was a great victory for friendliness among men when the colonies agreed to put away their jealousy and distrust of one another, and to make a common country.

Even when our fathers had joined together, and formed the United States of America, they were afraid of the people over the ocean. They were afraid of England, and believed that the English

LAFAYETTE.

We must remember that this great friend of Washington and of America had a long and very useful life in his own land, after he had devoted his youth to helping the cause of liberty over here.

stood ready to fight against them. We were a Republic, and our people were very suspicious of the monarchies of Europe, like Spain and Austria.

Most of our people at first were Protestants; they did not always remember what good patriots the Catholics of Maryland had been in the Revolution. A great many people in Europe, it must be confessed, were not friendly to America. Kings and princes and lords did not like the plan of our great Republic for the people. The Republic was an experiment, and many thought that it would never succeed.

Friendliness has been growing all over the world during the past hundred years. Where are any enemies of America over the seas? Travel about through Europe, and try to find our enemies. Wherever we Americans may go we are pretty sure of being treated kindly. Where are the kings and princes who really purpose to do any harm to America? In many countries the Americans are favorites of the people. Nearly all nations like to have the Americans come and spend their money amongst them.

It is true that Americans sometimes do what Frenchmen or Englishmen or Spaniards do not like. So Eastern people or Southern people sometimes do what Western or Northern people do not like. But we have learned not to hate and fight each other, although we now and then disagree. So the peoples over the seas and we in America do not intend to be enemies, although we sometimes differ or misunderstand each other.

Why is it that the people of the world have come

to be so much more friendly toward one another
than they used to be? One reason is that a great
many of us have relatives over the ocean. The

W. E. GLADSTONE.

This famous English prime-minister was a great lover of liberty,
not for his own people alone, but also for oppressed peoples in other
lands. He was a special friend of America.

English people are our cousins, more or less re-
moved. Others of us have had uncles or grand-

parents over in Ireland, or in the fatherland of Germany, or in Sweden or Italy. We cannot call that a foreign country where our relatives live. Neither can we quite call that a foreign country where the relatives of our own friends and neighbors and schoolmates live. For we all know Americans who came of the German or the Irish or some other national stock.

STEAMER LOADING GRAIN.

Who has ever seen such a queer building as this in the picture? It is a grain elevator. To what port or what country do you think that the steamer will sail?

Another reason why we grow friendly to the peoples over the seas is that there is so much trade and travel between the other countries and ours. Every big steamer that crosses the ocean weaves a thread that binds us all closer together. Our American wheat goes to feed the English workmen; our cotton goes to be made into cloth; fine goods come from the French and Belgian factories

to be displayed in the stores of New York and Chicago.   The great steamers carry thousands of letters,
—letters about business, friendly letters, and love

LAFAYETTE MONUMENT, WASHINGTON, D.C.

Let the pupils find out and tell all that they can about Lafayette.
Ought we not always to be great friends to the country that sent us
such a noble lover of liberty?

letters.   Men who get letters from one another, who
get money and supplies from the people over the

water—men in America who read French or German or Italian books and newspapers, come to feel

EDMUND BURKE.

This sturdy friend of America was born in Ireland. During the American Revolution he was a member of the British Parliament. He was fearless and eloquent in speaking whatever he believed to be true, or for the good of the people.

toward the men of Europe as the men in New England feel toward the men in Texas or California.

The truth is, we are becoming acquainted with
each other all over the world. We find that the
men in Europe or Asia are very much like us. We
all have the same human nature in us. We all like
to be treated fairly and kindly. We all feel pleas-
antly toward those who are just and generous to us.
Friendly people, whether they are Americans or
strangers, help us to be friendly too. Selfish people, whether they are relatives or foreigners, are
dangerous to us.

There are certain people over the seas who are
specially the friends of America. Most of the plain
working people in Europe are our good friends.
Why is this? It is because they believe, as we do,
in government for the people. They want such
government as we have, in Prussia and Austria and
Russia. In England the plain working people already have probably as much power as we have here.
That is, the government of England is becoming a
government for the whole people. The English people
are therefore our particular friends. Let us never forget that thousands of them were willing for our sakes
to suffer to the verge of starvation in the Civil War.[1]

---

[1] This was in the time of the " Cotton Famine." This war prevented
the Lancashire mills from getting their usual supply of cotton from
the South. There were Englishmen who wanted their government to
interfere and put a stop to the war so as to have plenty of cotton again.
But the Lancashire weavers said No. They loved America, and wished

There have always been many great friends of America among the leaders and statesmen and teachers and the best-educated men in Europe. The men and women who love liberty and hold high hopes of a better time to come, are sure to believe in America.

There were thousands of such true men in England who helped us mightily in the days of Washington and Franklin. The great William Pitt and the eloquent Burke were our friends. They held that our cause was the cause of England. They spoke for us and they voted for us in the British Parliament, as bravely as Samuel Adams and Patrick Henry spoke and voted here. Lafayette, the rich French nobleman, a Catholic, was the friend of America; and the German, Baron. Steuben.

We have great numbers of such good friends in Europe to-day. Some of them are rich and powerful. They are trying to gain for their own people the same great end that we aim to secure in America for every one of our children; namely, a fair chance to work out a noble and useful human life. Their cause is our cause. Let us never forget our friends over the seas. Let us never insult the flags that float over their heads. While we salute our own flag, let us sometimes salute the flags of other nations. For we are all one, — friends at heart, children of the Heavenly Father.

to put an end to slavery. Americans, North and South, are now one in their gladness that there are no longer slaves in the land. We can all join in praising the Lancashire workmen.

CHAPTER IX.

THE LAWS OF THE LAND.

LET us suppose something very strange. We will suppose that some day the master of the school should give notice that all the rules were suspended. Every one might do as he pleased for the whole morning; the scholars might get their lessons or not; they might recite or not; they might whisper and talk aloud; they might play games; they might make mischief if they chose; they might, if they liked, injure the books and desks; the stronger or careless boys might hurt the little ones. What do you think would happen in that school?

It is possible that some of the boys would like such a school for a day or two. But they would soon become tired of it. No one could possibly learn anything; no one could even read story-books in peace; the noise would be dreadful; the teacher would not be of the slightest use; the schoolhouse would not be half so good a place to play in as the playground is. In fact, to suspend all the rules would be like stopping the school. The children would go home and say to their parents, "We do not want to go to that school any longer; we cannot learn anything there."

Or, perhaps the older and brighter boys by the end of the third day would come to the master and say, "We wish that you would make a few rules for us."

"What rules shall I make?" the master might say. "Will you vote to make some rules for yourselves?"

RAILROAD TRAIN.

If this great engine keeps safely on the track, it will run many thousands of miles. But alas! if a careless switchman makes a mistake, or a faulty rail breaks.

"Yes," the boys would answer, "very willingly. We will vote to have decent order in the schoolroom. We will vote to stop the talking and the play. We will vote to give every fellow a fair chance to study in quiet. We will vote to have recitations again and not to let any one interrupt the lessons with noise. We will vote not only that the teacher ought to be here promptly on time when school begins, but that every

one of us ought also to be in his seat.   We will vote
that, as long as we go to school, no one can be absent
without some good reason."

"Very well," the master might reply, " I like your
rules.   They are just as good as my rules are.   Let
us call them *our* rules, and let us first vote for them,
and then let us all try to keep them."

BROOKLYN BRIDGE.

There were once "Seven Wonders of the Old World."   This
great suspension bridge over a mile long, and above the masts of
the ships, is one of the wonders of our New World.   Do not forget
the name of Roebling, the brave engineer, one of the heroes of peace,
who built this bridge in his thought.

We do not even like to guess what would happen
if all the laws of the land were suspended for a single week.   To be sure, most people would go on as
before, and behave themselves perfectly well.   But
a very few mischievous people might make a deal
of costly trouble.   What if half-crazy men should
get drunk and go through the streets firing revolvers

into the crowd? Or, what if mischief-makers should
set fire to buildings? No people that we have ever
heard of have tried the experiment of living without
any laws.

Where do our American laws come from? No
great master or king makes them and forces us to
keep them. No little committee of wise men tells
us common people that we must do what they bid
us. The laws are *our* laws. Some of them have
come down from very ancient times. Our forefathers used them for hundreds of years. They
seem so good and sacred that men have often rev-
erently said that "God taught them to men." The
law not to murder, the law not to steal, the laws to
keep ourselves pure, the laws not to injure our
neighbors — these are the laws of intelligent and
civilized men all over the world. We say that those
who do not keep these grand and ancient laws are
barbarians or savages.

Some of our laws have grown. There were new
needs, and new laws had to be made to meet these
needs. Thus, there were no laws about keeping the
streets clean till men found out that filthy streets
breed disease. There could have been no laws
about clearing the sidewalks of dust or rubbish in
the days, not so long ago, when men had no sidewalks in their cities. There were no laws about railroads till the age of steam came in.

All the laws, however they came, whether they are
old or new, are *our* laws. They belong to all the

people; they are for the sake of all of us, for the poor even more, if possible, than for the rich. We vote for the laws; or we vote for the men who make them; or we vote for the government that carries out and enforces the laws.

If any law happens not to seem to all of us quite fair, we can petition, like the scholars in a school, to have that law altered and made right. We can go to work and persuade others to join us in getting that law changed. But as long as the majority of the people vote to retain the law, no one has any selfish right to suspend it and make disorder and trouble for all the rest.

Along the low banks of the Mississippi River they build great embankments, or levees, to keep the waters from overflowing the land and sweeping away the farmer's crops and his buildings. Our laws are like the vast levees that curb the water of the river. Our laws defend our homes, our lives, our property. Whoever breaks a law is like the man who cuts the levee and lets the water rush through. The harm and the cost come upon all of us.

You see, good rules do not take away our liberty. When the school for a single day suspends all its rules freedom is taken away. No one any longer can possibly read or study; every one is forced to be disturbed. The rules restore liberty. It is not true liberty to be allowed to spoil the school. True liberty is to be free to enjoy the privileges of the school. It is liberty to be able in quiet to read, to write, to study, to recite lessons.

So in the city, it is liberty to be able to go about one's business and not to be disturbed by any one. It is liberty to be able to walk the streets without fear by night as well as by day. It is liberty to be able to display goods in the shop windows without danger of being robbed. It is liberty to be able to travel across the Continent to the Pacific Ocean, and to find protection wherever one goes. Our laws give us Americans this great liberty. The only demand made of us is that we obey the laws as we wish others to obey them.

Some laws are for our convenience. Thus, if we are driving in a carriage or riding a bicycle, there is a rule or law to turn to the right in meeting another vehicle. Suppose we had no law on our roads and one could go to the right or left as he liked. Do you not see at once how teams and riders would run into each other? Sometimes careless people think that they can break the rule "just once," and turn the wrong way. Or they venture to ride on crowded streets faster than the law allows. Many bad accidents happen to innocent persons, when selfish or reckless men dare to break the laws which are for the convenience and safety of all of us.

The laws are like the tracks on which the car-wheels run. As long as the car keeps upon its track it will run swiftly and safely.

CHAPTER X.

A GREAT city has thousands of policemen. They are like an army in Boston or New York or Chicago. Even the little cities and the towns have a force of policemen, or at least a few constables. All these policemen, with their officers and captains, must be paid for by the people. What are they for? What good do they do, that we should keep them in our pay?

Some one may answer: "The police are appointed to catch or arrest thieves and others who break the laws, and to bring them to court and, later, take them to jail. They run after boys who steal apples or pears, or who throw stones on the streets." But, if you should follow a policeman a whole day, it would often happen that he would not arrest or chase any one. He walks back and forth over his beat and no one offers to do any mischief.

"Yes," you will say, "but every one knows that the policeman is there, and bad men are afraid and keep out of his way." The rogues also know that the country is covered with policemen; so that if they did a crime in Philadelphia or Brooklyn, and escaped

73

to California, a telegraph message could go in a few moments to San Francisco to notify the police there to be on the watch and arrest them. Thus, all the policemen in the country help one another to defend the laws.

Yes, and if some very great wrong has been done, the police in Canada and over the ocean, in London or Paris, will also help our police at home to catch a dangerous man and keep him from doing harm to his fellows; for all the people in the world, who stand by the laws of justice, are friends and helpers to one another.

We must not think that the policemen are all the time looking for rogues. Most people are too sensible to be rogues and thieves, or to break the laws and get themselves into trouble. The policeman is on the watch wherever he goes, and especially in the night, for any sign of fire. If he sees anywhere a suspicious blaze or smoke, he finds out what it is. Sometimes he is able to put a fire out before it does any harm; sometimes he has to ring the alarm for the engines to come.

There are careless clerks who forget to lock up their stores at night. The policeman must try the doors and see that all is right. The policeman, you see, is really a watchman. If every one did right, and there were no longer thieves and robbers in the land, we should not need nearly so many policemen, but we should still require public watchmen in every great town.

There are many people who are not really wicked, but who become very careless. They forget to remove the ice from their sidewalks; they throw rubbish into the gutter; they keep nuisances, as, for instance, ugly dogs, on their premises, without thinking of their neighbors' comfort or safety; they drive, or ride bicycles, as if the whole street belonged to them. The policeman must look after these careless people; he must remind them of the rules of the city; he must report them if they continue to forget; sometimes it is necessary to arrest them, for a very careless man may do as much harm as if he were a bad man.

There is another part of the work of the police that many of us forget. Perhaps it is the pleasantest part of their work. They must help people who are in need or distress. If a little child loses its way, if any one meets with an accident or is taken sick, if a team breaks down, if a poor tramp is found by the roadside almost frozen to death, the policeman must lend a hand. Perhaps he will call for a physician, or he will telephone for help to the station house, or he will get the injured man into the hospital.

The good policeman is always ready also to answer the questions of citizens or strangers who need to be shown their way. If you did not know a single soul in a great city, the first policeman whom you met ought to befriend you and advise you where to go and what to do.

You will often see a policeman stationed at the crossing of a crowded street to keep the teams and cars in order, and to see that no woman or little child is run over. Or the policeman will stand at the doors of a great hall or theatre, and prevent the crowd from hurting one another. Thus the police help to preserve order and to keep the people safe from many kinds of danger.

We see now what kind of men we need for our

POLICEMAN.

police. In the first place, we need strong, healthy men, who can bear exposure to rain and snow, to summer heat and winter cold. We need brave men who are not afraid to stand alone in the night, who would die rather than desert their post; for the policemen are like sentinels on duty. A policeman must be thoroughly honest. He must be a man whom we all can trust. If he finds a purse full of money he must report it and try to discover the owner. He must be a man whom we could leave in charge of the keys to our houses, if we should go out of town. He must be perfectly truthful. How terrible it would be if the policeman was a liar or dishonest, that is, a traitor!

The policeman must also be a kind and friendly man. We have seen that one of his great duties is to look after little children, the infirm, the aged, those who need help. This calls for a gentle man, as well as a strong and brave man. But more than this, the policeman must be kind toward those who break the laws and have to be arrested. The law-breakers are human beings with feelings just like ours. If they have done wrong and have got into trouble, they are very much to be pitied. We wish them to be cured of doing wrong; we cannot bear to see any one ugly, harsh, abusive, and cruel to them. We wish the policeman to help them if he can. We do not wish him to arrest any one unless it is quite necessary and clearly his duty. We want him to keep people out of jail rather than to send them there.

Thus the policeman must be a friend to us all; he must be the friend and helper of those who obey the laws; and he must be a friend to those who do wrong, just as a doctor is a friend to the sick man, whom he has to confine to his bed.

CHAPTER XI.

ONE of the largest and most costly buildings in many a town is the court-house. Perhaps as the children pass by its doors they feel a sort of dread. Here people charged with crime are taken to be tried. Policemen or sheriffs are about its rooms, waiting upon the service of the laws. Judges and other officers are within; lawyers and witnesses are coming and going.

Not very far away from the court-house is the county jail or perhaps the State prison. The judge sentences guilty men and women to be shut up in its strong walls, sometimes for many years; in some cases for life. All this is very serious business.

Does any one think that the courts are only intended to try bad people and to deal out punishment to them? Does some one perhaps think that the judges and sheriffs are only for the sake of protecting the good and law-abiding citizens, and that they are the enemies of bad and disobedient people? This would be a great mistake. The fact is, the people who do wrong have rights. They have the

78

right to expect justice; that is, perfectly fair treatment. Though they have done harm, they are still men. They must be treated like men. How should we like to be treated if we had broken the laws?

We have now and then read in the papers, that some wretched man, perhaps out on the frontier or

COURT-HOUSE AND POST-OFFICE, DENVER, COL.

Do you know of any buildings like this in the picture, that are owned by the people of the United States? Does the Post-office where you live belong to the government?

in some half-savage part of the country, has been "lynched." What does that mean? It means that a band of men, being very angry on account of a crime that has been committed, — possibly the stealing of horses, — have pounced on their victim, and, without waiting for the officers of the law or for witnesses, have proceeded to hang the man at once. They very likely do this act, like cowards, at night. It may be that their victim was not the guilty person at all. If he was surely guilty, this was no excuse for cruelty and abuse. Ought not the man to have had a fair trial?

In old times it often happened that men were seized and thrown into a dungeon, without even being told what they had done to deserve imprisonment. Many a time innocent men have died in prison. In some countries to-day people are still liable to imprisonment without knowing who accuses them of doing wrong. Now the courts are intended to save innocent and guilty men alike from cruel and barbarous treatment. Men must not be lynched; they must know what charge is made against them; they must be brought out of jail and into the public court-room; if there is no reason to detain them they must be promptly set free. We in America do not believe that a man has done wrong until we are made sure of it. The courts must give every man justice, even if he is guilty.

The judge is not the enemy of the offender, but he is his friend. His duty is to see that the trial is perfectly fair. The prisoner cannot be convicted of guilt without the clear proof of truthful witnesses. All that can be said in his behalf must be heard and weighed. If he is poor and cannot hire a lawyer to speak for him, the judge must see to it that a

lawyer is appointed and paid for at public cost.
If he is proved guilty, the judge must still award his

JOHN MARSHALL.

This man was a noble patriot and a good friend of Washington.
He was an excellent lawyer and one of the best judges who ever
presided over our Supreme Court.

sentence with a view to the good of the prisoner. He must continue to be his friend and not his enemy.

The twelve jurymen who decide whether the prisoner is guilty or not, are also his friends and not his enemies. They promise solemnly to try to be perfectly fair. They listen to all the evidence so as to be sure not to do an injustice. They talk the whole case over by themselves, and unless they all agree that there is ample proof of the man's guilt he cannot be punished.

But how about the prison and the jailers? The prison may be likened to a hospital, and the jailers may be likened to the doctors and nurses. We say, if a patient is very ill, that it is not good for him to go out. What if he has an infectious disease like smallpox? He ought not to want to go out and carry the disease to others. What if he has leprosy? It is very hard, but he ought to be willing to be shut away by himself.

So we say about crime. Crime hurts us all. As long as a man carries about with him criminal habits, he ought not to wish to be let out of the hospital, — that is, the prison. It is no kindness to let a man go free to burn houses or kill or steal. The kindness is in keeping him from doing any harm ; kindness is in trying to cure him.

It must be confessed that we have not thought enough about curing our prisoners of their bad habits. But there are a few prisons in our country that are really hospitals for the wrong-doers. Such a prison-hospital is at Elmira, in the State of New York. The business of every one in charge of this great institution is to befriend the men who are sent there. The men are taught useful trades, and when they go out into the world again, they often become good and law-abiding citizens. By and by we will have no other kind of prisons or jails except such as do hospital work, to befriend and cure their inmates. But if any of them cannot be cured, should they ever be permitted to come out to do harm to innocent people?

The courts and the judges not only do justice in cases of wrong and crime. A large part of their work has nothing to do with crime or with dangerous people. Indeed, this class is not large in America; for most of us mean to do right. But there are always hard questions that come up between neighbors, and between business men, and even between friends. There are questions about property and land and bargains, and the keeping

JOHN JAY.

Jay was a New York patriot. He helped make the treaty of peace after the War of the Revolution. Later he helped make another important treaty with England. Washington appointed him to be the first Chief Justice of the United States.

of promises. Sometimes men misunderstand each
other. Often they only see their own side of a question, and do not see their neighbor's side. Often each
man is confident that he is right and the other is
wrong. Sometimes both men are wrong, or they are
each partly wrong and partly right. Their questions
are like those which arise between boys at their
games. The boys need an umpire to decide for
them. So the men need courts and judges.

It is costly business to quarrel or dispute and to
pay lawyers' bills. It is a great deal better to be
fair-minded, and to try to see how the case looks
to the other side. It is sometimes better to get out
of a quarrelsome man's way altogether, and not to do
any more business with him. Yes, it may be better
to let him have more than his share, rather than to
stop and dispute. It is costly also to the public, that
is, to all of us, to keep so many courts open where
men may go to have their cases tried. But it would
be a great deal worse and far more costly if every
man undertook to settle his own case, and to compel
his neighbor by force to do him justice. Where men
have courts, they learn to treat each other like gentlemen, even when they are obliged to differ.

What kind of men do we need for judges, and for
jurors too? We need fair men, who can see both
sides and all sides of a question. We need kind and
friendly persons, who are never hard upon a man
because he is down. We want faithful men, who
will take great pains to find out all that is possible

before they make a decision, who will give the same
attention to the poor as to the rich. We need well-
trained judges who know what the laws are. We
want fearless judges, who will do justice, even when
their decision is not popular; for sometimes a judge
has to stand up all alone and decide against people's
prejudices and against his own wishes also. The
judge must not have favorites. He must be as strict
with his own neighbors as with any stranger, with his
countrymen as with foreigners. He must be beyond
the reach of a bribe; he must never make the gain
of a dollar for himself by means of his decision.

Do we need just, friendly, conscientious, and brave
men also for lawyers? Of course we do. What are
the lawyers for, unless to help the courts to do justice? What a shame it would be if lawyers used the
courts to help rascals escape, or to cheat honest men
out of their property! There are countries where
the courts still aid the oppressors to wrong the people. Let us never forget that in America the courts
are for the defence of the people.

CHAPTER XII.

LET us suppose that we should ask all the men and women whom we know, "What is your business?" We should not go far before we found some one who would answer, "I work for the city," or, "I work for the town." Of course the teachers work for the towns or the cities, and they are paid out of the town or city money. The policemen and sheriffs and the judges also work for the people, that is, for all of us, and the people must pay them their salaries.

But there are a great many others who work for the people. Especially in a great city, you will be surprised at the number of men who have something to do with the city work. There must be a force of firemen, night and day, ready to tend the steam fire-engines and the hose carriages. There must be men at work keeping the streets in order and building new streets. There must be pavers and bricklayers and workers in asphalt. Another set of men must be at work all the time in the parks and public gardens, or these beautiful places for the people would soon look shabby and go to waste. There must be another force of men working to keep the city clean, sweeping the streets, and removing ashes and refuse and garbage. Others must build and repair the great sewers.

What does the town or city need in great quantities? It needs a plentiful supply of pure water. There must be enough to sprinkle the streets, and keep the grass fresh, and to fill all the factory

FIRE-ENGINE ON ITS WAY TO A FIRE.

boilers. There must be enough to play in the fountains. A force of men is therefore needed all the time to work in the water department; to lay mains and pipes and keep them in repair; to build and maintain reservoirs, or lakes of clear water, far back among the hills.

The city must have hospitals also for its sick, and homes for the aged and poor and for orphan children. It must have doctors and nurses; it must have superintendents or overseers, and engineers and clerks and typewriters. It wants skilful men and women to fill all kinds of offices. You can probably think of some of its servants whom we have not yet mentioned at all.

What are all these town and city offices for? There are some people who think that the city

GARDENERS AT WORK IN THE PUBLIC GARDEN, BOSTON.

Do you suppose that these men are doing as good work in this public garden as they would do in their own gardens? Ought they to do as good work for the people as they would do for themselves?

work is for the men and women who draw their pay for doing it. What a fine thing, they say, it would be to get city work, and to have short and easy hours, and to be sure of good pay every week. They really think that the work is all made for the sake of the office-holders. But this surely is not a good American idea about the work of the city. What, then, is the American idea about this work?

A good American holds that all the city work is for the sake of the people. The men on the streets are not there to draw pay, but to do their very best to make good streets. If a man were working for his brother, would he not think it mean business to waste material and make a slovenly job? Would he not

CONGRESSIONAL LIBRARY.

Every boy and girl in the United States ought sometime to go to Washington, and to see this magnificent Library that belongs to us all. It is on the Capitol Hill.

think it mean if his brother were paying him wages, to dawdle away his time? Then is it not mean likewise to waste the people's money and material, or to dawdle away the time that men owe to their own city?

The same rule holds with the city doctors and architects and engineers. They do not serve the city in order to draw their salaries, but to help the city;

to fight off disease, to plan the best possible buildings, to save the people of their city from needless
waste and expense. Suppose a boy is chosen captain

WILLIAM PENN.

This man is dressed like a soldier. But he was really one of the
bravest lovers of peace. If every one had treated the Indians as
fairly as Penn, there never would have been an Indian war. Which
State did he found?

of his base-ball nine. Why is he made captain? Is
it only as an honor to the boy? Is it for the boy's
sake, or is it wholly for the sake of the club?

So we say of all the city officers. We do not choose them for their sake, but we choose them and pay them salaries for the sake of the people. Who is strong, able, and honest, so as to give us the very best and most faithful service? He is the man whom we want for a fireman, or a driver, or a mason, or a laborer. Who is in the city work to get as much as he can out of the city and to do as little as possible for his pay? He is a kind of cheat, and even a traitor. Suppose he is a health officer, and his carelessness lets disease and death get into the city. Suppose his bad work on the streets causes an accident, and some one is lamed for life in consequence.

We have called the men and women who do town or city work the public servants. Is *servant* a good name to use for them? Is not a servant one who does rather mean work? Would a lady or gentleman like to be called a "servant"? We take this word *servant*, because it is the best word to tell the truth.

All who do the city work *serve* the city. To serve is what they are for. Is not this what any good and honest citizen would like to do? Would you not wish, if you could, to do something handsome for the city, that is, for your own people? Would you not like to give them honest, effective work, so good that it would never need to be done again? Would you not be ashamed if your work was not worth as much as it cost? Would you rather not be paid too little, and so leave the city better for your work, than be paid too much and so defraud the people?

The truth is, all the men whom the world honors most have loved to be thought of as public servants. The great Hebrew teachers, Moses and Isaiah, the noble Christian teachers, Jesus and Paul, Catholics like Joan of Arc and Thomas More, and Protestants such as William Penn and Gladstone, have been noble examples to show that the best kind of man is not here in this world to get place and honor and pay, "to be ministered unto," but to be a minister ; that is, a servant of the people, so as to help make the world happier, richer, and better.   To do this is the true American idea of life.

CHAPTER XIII.

THE MAYOR, OR THE HEAD SERVANT.

OVER in London there is a famous palace, called the Mansion House, where the Lord Mayor lives. Within the bounds of the city he is held to be next in rank to the king or queen. If you should see him in all the splendor of his dress on some grand holiday, perhaps you would not guess what the real business of the mayor is. You would imagine that he had no business or work, but that his office was to preside over great festivities, and to sit at the head of a rich banqueting hall. But the real duty of the Lord Mayor of London is not to dress in gay robes and to assist at great dinners. He is in fact the head servant of the people of the city of London, of the poor as truly as of the rich. It is the duty of the mayor of a city to oversee the vast work that goes on for the health, the safety, the welfare, and the happiness of all the people. Perhaps some of the Lord Mayors of London have forgotten for what they are chosen, but we do not intend here in America to let our mayors ever forget what great and hard work we expect of them.

Whenever hundreds or thousands of men are at

work, there must be a head or captain, just as there must be a general over an army. Some one must plan for the men and show them what to do. We have seen not only that a city has many men and women in its employ, but also that it has various branches or departments of work, — the police, the water, protection against fire, the public health, the schools, and so on. There must be some one to oversee the working of all these branches of the public service. It might happen that the men of the street department would think that their work was the most important, and would want to spend more than the city could afford in improving the streets.

The mayor's business is to watch over the best interests of all the departments, so that the firemen and the sewer men have their fair share of the supplies, as well as the men in care of the streets and of the parks. It may be that the people at the east end of the town want a great deal of money to give their part of the city a new park. The mayor will wish to do all that he can for the park, but he wishes also to be sure that the boys and girls at the south end shall have playgrounds or a bathing-house.

It may be that the merchants ask the city to help their business by cutting a new thoroughfare through the heart of the town, while at the same time the attention of the mayor is called to the untidy houses where multitudes of poor people are crowded. The mayor is as much the servant of the poorest citizen as of the richest. He must do his best for all.

It may be that the men who own saloons desire freedom to sell liquor, while other men and women wish to forbid all selling of liquor in the city. The mayor must hear both sides, and he must obey and enforce the laws, even if men speak against him and threaten to turn him out of office. The mayor has not power enough to alter the laws; he must obey them like any other man.

Men will come to the mayor seeking to get work from the city and to have places and salaries. The mayor's friends will wish him to favor them, or to help their sons and daughters with his influence. Men who have voted for the mayor will think that he owes them something, and that he may get them a job from the city in payment of their help in electing him mayor. He must not be the mayor for his friends or for his own party, but for the whole city and all the people. He cannot honestly appoint any person to an office, unless he really thinks that person is fitted to do the best kind of service for the city. Would the captain of the base-ball nine appoint his best friend to be catcher unless his friend was also the most skilful boy on the nine for that place?

Who is the firmest, bravest man of whom we can think? We often imagine it is a soldier or sailor, — Dewey or Hobson or Roosevelt. But the mayor of a city needs not less, but even more, firmness of nerve, courage, and will than any general or commodore. Mayors have sometimes had to stand at the head of the police and to face a crazy mob, to quiet angry or

suffering men, and to save bloodshed.   Mayors have
often to do harder things : they must say No to their

STATUE OF JOSIAH QUINCY, MAYOR
OF BOSTON, 1823-1828.

This man was mayor, not for
his own sake, for pay, or for the
honor, but for the good of the
people. The people honored him
for this, and his statue stands as a
memorial before the City Hall.
Why should not every mayor be
like Quincy ?

own   friends;   they
must sometimes de-
cide against their own
party for the sake of
the public good ; they
must sometimes for-
bid bad and wasteful
use of the people's
money ;   they   must
turn   out   unfaith-
ful officers, and pos-
sibly make enemies
in   so   doing; they
must even speak out
and refuse the people,
if ever the people de-
mand an illegal or
wrong   thing;   they
must run the risk of
being unpopular for
the sake of the public
good ; they must al-
ways be ready and
willing to give up
office and go back
to the ranks, and take

the place of private citizens, if the people have no
further use for them.

Only a very brave man therefore can be a faithful and honest mayor.   But when once the people have found such a man there is no one whom they respect and love more.   Show them that their mayor is not in office for the honor or the pay, for his friends or for his party, but to serve the people; show them that he is not afraid of anybody, that he is fair and impartial, that he treats rich and poor alike on the ground of their common manhood, that he is as kind and friendly as he is upright and firm, — and the people cannot do too much for this kind of mayor.

Have there ever been mayors like this, — true, sincere, fearless, public-spirited ?   Yes, the city of Boston had such a mayor once under the honored name of Josiah Quincy ; New York had its Mayor Hewitt ; Brooklyn had its Mayor Low ; Detroit had its Mayor Pingree ; Buffalo had its Mayor Cleveland, who, because he did good service as mayor, was afterward intrusted with the presidency of the nation.   There have been many mayors in many cities in the Old World and in America whom the people have had a right to trust.   They have been men who held that their sole business was to serve the people.   Is it not pitiable that schoolboys should ever grow up to betray the people for the sake of their own ambition or in order to enrich themselves ?   Is it not a splendid chance that our American boys have to become men whom after-generations will honor and thank for their honest public service in helping to build up and beautify noble cities ?

CHAPTER XIV.

THE CITY FATHERS, OR KEEPING HOUSE FOR THE PEOPLE.

A CITY or town is like a great house, under the roof of which thousands of people are living. They must have all kinds of supplies; they must have rules or laws, so as not to interfere with each other or do injustice. There will often be puzzling questions to decide, just as when a father and mother have to decide about painting their house, or building an ell, or sending their boy to college. We say when the parents have a home of their own and buy their provisions, and take care of their house, and settle all kinds of questions about the family, that they are housekeepers. So we might say that the people in their great multitude of homes and stores and shops, all bound together by common streets, with their various companies of public servants, are "house-keepers" together for the city.

As long as people live in a little town, or in the country, the public housekeeping is simple, and does not take much time. Once or twice a year all the people, or all the men, can come together and hear what their selectmen and school committee advise,

and talk over their town business, and choose officers
for the year, and decide what is for the good of the
town.　Perhaps all this business will not take more
than three or four hours.　But in a big town or a
city there is too much business to be done in this easy

CITY HALL, NEW YORK.

The business of one of our great cities is larger than all the business of the kingdom of France or England was, only a few hundred
years ago.　The City Hall, where the people's business goes on,
is a sort of palace full of rooms and offices.

fashion.　If all the fathers of all the children in Boston or Chicago or New York tried to get together in
one place to talk over the city business, no building
would be large enough to hold them.　They would
need also to meet every week, and perhaps every

day in some weeks, to get through with the immense housekeeping of their city.

What simple and fair plan for deciding all the multitude of questions about the welfare of the city can we think of? Suppose that, instead of bringing all the people together to hear reports about the needs of the city, and to decide what we will do, we select a few of the best and wisest men among our neighbors and fellow-citizens. Suppose we intrust to them the duty of acting for us. Suppose that, instead of making rules for ourselves in a big town meeting, we charge these few men to make our rules for us, and that we agree to abide by whatever they do. Suppose that we agree to spend the money which they say is needful to keep our city in order. This seems to be a fair plan, and it is exactly what almost all large towns or cities have to do. We sometimes call the men whom we choose to act for all of us "the City Fathers."

Sometimes these men are called Aldermen, from an old English word that means the *Elders*. But this does not mean that our aldermen have to be old men. They may be as young as thirty years, or younger. They are often called Councilmen, for they counsel together.

A city may have two sets of counsellors, — a larger body, as large in some cases as seventy or more, and a smaller number of perhaps only twelve men. In such cities both bodies must agree before anything can be done. Indeed, often the public business suffers because the two bodies do not work well together.

You must know that City Councils do not carry on the city business themselves. They only hold meetings to talk about the business and to settle the questions that the people are too busy to settle themselves.

They make various rules for the welfare of the city; they decide what new streets shall be laid out, or what new buildings shall be erected for the city; they help to shape the business which the mayor and the other servants of the people must carry out. As parents decide to spend their money and, for instance, to build a new bath-room, and then employ a carpenter and a plumber to do the work for them, so the City Fathers, that is, the aldermen, set their various officers to work, as they think the needs of the city demand.

How can any one man know enough to decide the thousand questions that arise about a growing city, — questions about health, about the best materials for pavements, about the right kind of schoolhouses? The men on the City Council help each other by dividing their work; they make up little committees among themselves; one committee will take the streets in hand, another will take charge of the public buildings, another may find out what other cities are doing for public parks. Each committee will make a report to the whole Council and advise what is best to be done.

Is the mayor, then, a sort of servant of the City

Council? Yes. But in truth every member of the Council is really a servant too. He is a servant of the people, and he is also a servant to the other members of the Council. If they direct one of their number to inspect the wharves of the city, or to go to another city for information about pavements, he must be ready to serve and must report the facts which the Board or Council needs to know.

The mayor, however, is a head servant over the aldermen. An alderman might wish to spend money for his own ward, or his end of the city. He might be thinking of what his own neighbors would like to get out of the city. The mayor, as we have seen, is the servant of the whole city and all the people. Whatever the aldermen decide, the mayor must think it over and decide whether it is for the best good of the city.

If a new rule, or a vote to spend the city money, does not seem right to the mayor, he must tell the aldermen his objections, and they must talk about it again and make up their minds whether they wish to pass it against the judgment of their mayor. If they do pass it again, as many as two-thirds of them must agree to this. Thus the mayor sometimes is able to thwart or veto the will of the City Council. If the mayor approves the new rule, or the proposed outlay of the city money, a bare majority, that is, one more than half of the City Council, — for example, thirteen men out of a Board of twenty-four, — may decide the matter. But if the mayor says No, it will need as many as sixteen men out of the twenty-four, to carry out the same plan.

What sort of men ought to be chosen to do the housekeeping of the city? Suppose that we should carelessly choose quite young and inexperienced men, — boys just out of college, or ignorant men, or those who had mismanaged their own business and wasted their own money. Suppose that we should choose dishonest men, who were not ashamed to steal the public money for themselves and their friends. Suppose that we should choose men who could not keep sober and whom the boys and girls could not respect.

What should you think if parents appointed a committee of young boys to take charge of building a new house? The people have often been so good-natured and careless as to trust their great housekeeping, with millions of dollars of expense, to men who thought it fun to spend the city money. The money has therefore been wasted and often stolen; buildings have been ugly that might have been beautiful; work has had to be done over again; people have had to drink unwholesome water; the public health has suffered; children have died whose lives might have been saved; every one has had to pay more money for rent and taxes, — all because foolish and selfish men have sat in the chairs of the City Fathers.

There is one grand remedy for public waste and foolishness. It is the choice of true and unselfish men to manage the affairs of the people. The children in

our public schools will soon have this remedy in their
hands. Some of them in a few years will be sitting
in the council chambers of our cities all over the
land. The boys, and perhaps the girls, will soon be
voting for aldermen and councilmen. The children
are learning now which of their schoolmates are
honest and true. They are finding out if any boy
or girl is tricky and mean. The boys and girls who
love their city or town are not going to help choose
mean and selfish and tricky aldermen. They are not
going to be so foolish as to see their city money
wasted and their city robbed. The boys who are
reading these chapters, if ever they are made aldermen themselves, are not going to be false with the
people's money or to use it to "feather their own
nests."

CHAPTER XV.

THE COUNTRY PEOPLE.

A great many of the boys and girls of the United States never see a mayor. They do not live in a city, but in small villages or on farms in the country. The little villages and the scattered farms do not need many public officers or servants to take care of them. Each man has his own well or cistern. If a house catches fire the neighbors run to help put the fire out. The country people do not need parks and costly buildings. If some of their fellow-citizens are sick or poor, kind neighbors can generally look after their wants.

In the country, therefore, a few men can attend to all the public business, such as the care of the roads and the schools and of very poor and helpless neighbors. In some of the States, in all of the New England States, for example, selectmen are chosen every year to do the business of the town. There are commonly three selectmen. They do not need to give all their time to the town, and they are only paid a small salary. Indeed, many men are willing to give their service to their town for much less than

they could get for it from a bank or a railroad. This
is because they love their own town and take pleasure
in seeing it prosper. Besides the selectmen there
are only a few officers, a clerk to keep the records
and to give licenses, as, for example, when people are
married; a treasurer to keep and pay out the town
money, a school committee, perhaps a superintendent
or overseer of the highways, one or two constables or
policemen, and a few others, whom every boy or girl
who lives in a town will soon hear of.

Children will sometimes hear about counties, and
the county business. Their school is in a certain
county. Towns are only a few miles wide, perhaps
five or six miles. But counties are twenty-five or
forty or more miles across. In each county there is
a court-house, where the people at regular times may
find one of their judges ready to try cases at law, and
to sentence guilty persons to punishment.

In some of the States of our Union there are no
townships or selectmen, but the people manage all the
business of their roads and schools by the help of
county officers. There is a committee or commission
chosen by the people somewhat like the selectmen
of a town, to take charge of county affairs. Other
officers also, like those who serve in a town, are
chosen to keep the records, to keep the people's
money, and to serve the convenience of the people.
Most of these officers do not need to give all their
time to the public business, and they receive very
small salaries.

Many of the people of the United States frequently move from one place to another. Possibly they move about too often. People born and reared in the country go to a city to live. City people sometimes go into the country. It is easy to move from one State to another, for one may find friends everywhere. If one is ready to work and is fair and

THE PUBLIC LIBRARY, BOSTON.

This beautiful building stands in a grand square, facing a great church and close to the Art Museum. It is dedicated to the use of the people forever. Whoever comes to Boston is welcome to enjoy it.

kind, and especially if one knows how to do his work skilfully, he may be sure of a welcome wherever he goes.

Throughout the United States the laws are much the same; the methods of government are nearly alike. If a country boy has learned about his town or county, he will soon understand how a city ought to be managed.   He will find differences of method, or machinery, between one place and another.   A town government is like a very simple machine with only a few parts.   A city is like a great machine with many wheels and cogs and pieces.   Whoever uses the simple machine skilfully can soon learn how to handle the larger and more costly machine.   In every case more depends upon the skill of the men in charge than upon the machine itself.

Shall our great cities have good officers, wise and brave mayors, and honorable and public-spirited councilmen? The cities not only depend on their own children whom they are now educating in their schools to become good citizens, but they depend also upon the country boys and girls to furnish them with plenty of skilled hands to manage their business. The cities have no room for idle and shiftless people to move into them, but they always have room for the men and women of energy and character.

History is full of the stories of men who were born in the country and have made their way to great places of honor in famous cities.   Who has not heard of Dick Whittington, five hundred years ago, who, when his father died, at only thirteen years of age, went up to seek his fortune in London, and was made the Lord Mayor before he was forty?

Sturdy country boys have always carried vigor and courage into the city life. Ask who the most useful men are in the city of New York or Chicago, — merchants, physicians, architects, skilled workmen,

the leaders of their fellows; the chance is that they
were once country boys. You will often be shown

GOVERNOR ANDREW.

Here was a man who never fought a battle, but he was just as
brave as the soldiers, whom he helped to send to the front in the
time of the Civil War. He was kind and friendly to every one, and
the people of Massachusetts loved him.

the little farmhouse where some well-known man like

Governor Andrew of Massachusetts was born. Perhaps you will be shown the fine public library that a generous city man has erected as a gift to his native town. Yes! the cities always look to the country for their best men and women.

The children who read this little book can ask their fathers or older friends to tell them who are their own town or county officers. They can find out what these various officers do. They can ask especially what officers are serving the people as good public servants ought, not for the sake of the pay, but in order to do the most honest and faithful work for all of us. They can remember the names of such good public officers, and make up their minds, when they are old enough to have a voice in the people's business, what kind of officers they will help to choose.

If they ever hear of dishonest and unfaithful public servants, who waste or misuse or even steal the money of the people, the children will resolve to try to put a stop to such mischief. They can all resolve if ever, when they are grown up, the people wish to choose them for the public servants, that they will give their very best work for the people. They will, if possible, do a little better for the people's business than they would do for themselves. For when a man makes a mistake in his own business he perhaps hurts himself alone ; but when he abuses the public business he hurts himself and all the people besides.

When a boy is practising in throwing a ball by

himself, it is not very important if he sometimes fails to catch it; but when he is playing a match game, his failure may spoil the score for his side. So it is when a man turns aside from his own business and undertakes to serve the public. All his mistakes and failures now become a public loss. How shall we praise too highly the man in office who does his work for the sake of all of us better, if possible, than he does his own work? Such able and faithful public officers do good to all the people. Who of us is not richer for knowing some brave, skilful, kind, and honest public servant? How many men do we know of this sort?

CHAPTER XVI.

How do men become mayors and aldermen in the cities, or selectmen in the towns? In other words, how do we get leaders and managers for the people?

In old times the strongest and boldest men made themselves lords over the people. They got soldiers together, and they fought and killed those who resisted them. When the lord of a town died, his oldest son would take the rule and keep it, if he could, for his son after him. In the old countries of the world, in Italy or in Germany, you still are shown the castles, often on a high hill over the town, where the lords lived with their soldiers. Their business mostly was to fight against the lords of other cities. They did not care much how their poor people got on, who often suffered terribly from hunger and oppression, and were compelled to pay their money to the great lord upon the hill. Little did the lords trouble themselves in the old cruel days whether the children of their people ever learned to read and write.

Perhaps a king or emperor who lived in Paris, or Vienna, or St. Petersburg, thought that he owned all the cities of the realm. He could appoint his own friends or his sons to be the lords of the cities, and if the people did not like to be governed in this way they could not help themselves.   There are many parts of the world where the people have no voice at all in choosing who their mayors or public servants shall be.   The people are thought to live for the sake of

INDEPENDENCE HALL, 1776.

This was the old State House of Pennsylvania. Here the Declaration of Independence was proclaimed, and the bell in the tower rang out the glad news. Here, after the war, the convention of famous men sat who drew up the Constitution of the United States.

their lords and kings, instead of the kings and the mayors living for the people.

Over here in America we do not allow any man to seize the government for himself.   However strong and brave and wise a man is, even if he is as good as Washington was, we hold that he must never take

any office, till the people choose him of their own
free will. We hold also that every officer of ours
must be ready to lay down his office whenever his
term of office runs out. Even the President of the
United States must not hold his place for more than
four years, and then the people must say whether
they wish him to serve them longer. The mayors
and the aldermen often have to be chosen anew every
year. Of course it seems to us Americans very ridicu-
lous that any man should have the power to give his
office to his son, or to one of his relatives. The place
is not his, we say, but *ours* to bestow. What if his
son should happen to be foolish, or selfish, or bad ?

The business of choosing our officers, the mayors
and aldermen and others, we call *voting*. An election
day is appointed, perhaps once a year, when the people (that is, in most States, the men who are over
twenty-one years old) meet in their wardrooms or
polling-booths or town halls; printed papers or ballots are provided for them with the names of their
candidates, that is, the men or women who are
thought to be fit for the various offices.[1] Each voter
picks out the paper or ballot that contains the names
of the men he wants to elect; if he cannot find the
names printed of those whom he wishes to vote for,
he can write their names upon the paper himself.

---

[1] There are offices, for example on school committees, for which
women are specially fitted. Many men can see no reason why women,
as intelligent as themselves, ought not to be permitted to vote everywhere, as the men do.

Then he puts his ballot into a box; and when all the ballots are in, there are persons to count them carefully and to find out which names have the larger number of votes. Whoever in the city has more votes than any one else for the office of mayor is declared the mayor-elect. So with the other officers. Does not this way seem perfectly fair? Would it

VOTING-PLACE IN KANSAS, 1855.

This is a picture of what might have been seen before Kansas was made a State. There were wild times in Kansas when men were trying to decide whether it should be a slave State or free.

not be very wrong if any one could be made mayor whom the larger part of the people did not want?

Many of our States use what is called the Australian ballot. It is called so because it was used in Australia before we took it up. The names of all the different candidates are printed upon the same paper, and the voter marks a cross (X) against the names that he chooses. It often takes a large sheet to contain all the names. The voter must mark his ballot within a little enclosed box or desk, so that no one can see what names he marks. This rule is made so that every one can be quite free to vote as he thinks right. For no one has any business in America to tell another man how he must vote.

Suppose that the teacher were to ask all the scholars in the room to hold up their hands and vote whether they would take an extra lesson in arithmetic. Perhaps some of the children would look around to see how the others were going to vote. Some might vote so as to get favor with the teacher. But suppose that all the scholars voted Yes or No on bits of paper, and no one knew what any one else wrote. Then the teacher would find out exactly what the children really wished about the extra lesson. The Australian ballot works in this way. The voter does not have to think whether his vote will please his neighbors or his employer.

How can the people really know who is the best man in all the city to choose as their mayor, or who will make the best school committee? Most of us know only a few of our neighbors, and out of all whom we know there may not be one man who is wise enough to manage the affairs of a great city. The fathers of the pupils may be good men, and yet they may not have had any experience in managing the business of a city. The truth is, most of the people do not know, without being told by others, whom to choose as their mayor.   Most men have to make up their minds by what they hear and by reading the newspapers.   This is one reason why every voter needs to know how to read.

There are generally two or three parties into which nearly all the people are divided.   The men of each party hold meetings before every election.   Such a meeting is called a caucus.   Thus men really vote before the voting day, so as to see whom the party will try to elect.   You have all heard the rather long names of some of these parties: Democrats, Republicans, Populists, Prohibitionists, the Citizens' Party.

FEDERAL BUILDING, 1789.

On the balcony of this building on Wall Street, in New York City, Washington was inaugurated as the first President of the United States.

After the various parties have chosen their candidates, the people have a chance to inquire what kind of men they are.   The newspapers tell us about them, where they were born, what schools they went to, what their business has been, whether they have done good, honest service for the people or not.   Sometimes different papers tell opposite things about the same man.   But generally, if a man is true and faithful and a good friend to the people, you can tell whether he can be trusted to hold office.

It would not be possible, however, for the people to find out the character of all the officers who must serve them in a great city. We do not therefore try to vote for all. We do not vote for the captains of the police force, or for the men in the fire department, or for the clerks in the city hall. We charge the mayor alone, or the mayor and the aldermen, with the duty of appointing for us the best men whom they can find to serve us in most of the city business. Neither do we every year turn out the captains of the city work-men, or the men who keep the money and the accounts at the city hall. If they are good men, the longer they serve us the better they become; they get prac-tice and experience; whereas new and green hands would be just as wasteful in the city as they would be in a mill, or in a store or shop.

Therefore we say to the mayor: see to it that the business of all the city shall be well done; if any men are not doing their part well, appoint better men in their place; but if you find good men in office, keep them as long as you can. Is not this best for all the people, who are too busy to stop and find out for themselves about all the men in the pay and service of their city?

You can suppose that all the pupils in a school once a month chose their own monitors and a presi-dent for every class. You can suppose that the boys chose their most skilful fellows to play as a

school nine, or to make up a foot-ball team. How
would you like it if a little group of some of the
most selfish boys and girls in the school tried to get
themselves elected to the offices? What if some one,
instead of waiting to see whether the class really
wished him to be its president, bribed the younger
ones with candy and soda-water and so got the
election without deserving it? Would this be a real
and true honor? Or, worse yet, suppose the captain
of the school team got himself chosen by bullying the
little boys, or by treating his fellows, while the best
player, being a modest boy, was set aside. Would
not the boys be very indignant when they found out
that they had been imposed upon in this way?

It happens often that the people of a city are
imposed upon in the same way. The salaries and
the wages paid to the men who do the city work
are not too large for thorough and skilled men.
But this pay looks very large to incompetent persons who are thinking of the salary instead of thinking about the work to be done. There are always
some such men who try to get the offices and the
pay for themselves and for their friends. Sometimes
they do a very base thing: they give money and bribe
the voters to elect them; or they contrive to elect
careless men who will appoint them to fill the offices
in return for their help in the election.

Let us trust that these men do not quite know how
much harm all this does to the public service, and
how waste and expense thus come upon the poor;

for if there is bad government, the poor are likely to suffer more than the rich. Indeed, it costs more for every one to live in a badly managed city, just as it costs more to pay the bills in a badly managed house or hotel.

We can suppose that we all owned shares in a great Atlantic liner. Should we choose the captain merely because he was our friend, or rather because he was the ablest seaman to steer his ship over the sea? Should we choose a chief engineer who knew nothing about the care of the mammoth engine? Not if he were the jolliest good fellow in the world. Should we let landsmen pick out the crew of our ship, or should we not rather insist that the captain should choose his own crew? Should we respect the captain himself, if he got his place by promising to take as his mate one of the owners of the ship who knew nothing at all about sailing the ocean?

But a city is greater than any ship. The lives and happiness of many more people depend upon the skill, the character, the good-will, the fidelity of the officers of a city, than upon the captain and crew of any ship. The passengers of a ship may take only one short voyage in her. But people may live all their days in one city. The lives of a whole army of children are in the hands of the men who steer a great city. Are not the people very foolish if they vote for the wrong men, instead of taking pains to find whom they can trust?

CHAPTER XVII.

WE have seen that we all own together a great deal of property, — houses and lands and machines and horses and wagons. The town or the city also has large sums of money. One of our officers is a treasurer. In some cities he is chosen or voted for by the people on election day. In others he is appointed by the mayor. His duty is to take charge of all the people's money, to pay it out when the town or city needs to purchase supplies, and to keep a careful account of every dollar.

The treasurer must be perfectly honest. He must not have any temptation to take any of the people's money intrusted to him. He must not think of borrowing any of this money for himself, even if he could pay it back twice over. This money is a trust, and a treasurer therefore has to be more careful of it than he is of his own money.

The treasurer must not only be honest; he must be entirely accurate, he must not make any blunders or mistakes, he must count correctly, and he must never forget to put down in his books every smallest item of money that comes in or goes out. No careless person can ever be a good treasurer, not even if he is honest. The treasurer of the people's money must also be brave; he must never be persuaded, or frightened, or forced to give up the money in his charge. If a faithful watch-dog will lay down his life for the protection of his master's house, so will a good

U. S. TREASURY BUILDING, WASHINGTON, D.C.

Here are many offices and a little army of clerks and book-keepers. In the basement are great vaults or safes, filled with the people's money. "Uncle Sam" must set a good example to his people and pay all his bills exactly as he promised.

treasurer die if need be in guarding the people's property.

He must also be courteous and kindly in his manner. Like the mayor, he stands for the people, and must show himself worthy of them. He must be sure to treat men as men, whether they are rich or poor; whether they are dressed in good clothes or in shabby clothes.

The treasurer may have a number of men and women to help him in his office, to collect money, and to keep big account books. They must also be, like the treasurer, honest, accurate, trustworthy, and civil to everybody. One thing for which the good scholars in arithmetic and bookkeeping in our schools are being fitted, is to make the kind of men and women who can be trusted to keep the money of the city.

What does the city or town do with its public money? You can easily guess. A good deal of it goes at once to pay for keeping the schools open. It goes also for paying the salaries of policemen, and firemen, and all the men and women who do work for the people, or in other words, the public work that we all club together to pay for. Indeed, we could hardly do it at all, unless we agreed to pay for it together. How could we otherwise get a supply of pure water from the distant streams or springs, and bring it into all the narrow streets of the town? Or, how could we lay great sewer pipes and carry away all the refuse from our homes? These things cost a great deal of money. Most of the people are too busy and too poor to do such things for themselves; and, therefore, all the citizens agree or vote to spend the public money to make the city clean, healthy, safe, and comfortable.

Should you not think that the cities and towns

would become poor by spending millions of dollars of the people's money every year? They would become poor if this money went, as in the old days, to the support of great lords and kings, living in their palaces, and lavishing the money upon themselves and their favorites. Our cities suffer now, as we have seen, if selfish men waste or steal their money.

But we intend to lay out our public money so that every one will be richer and better off. If the roads and streets are good, all the teamsters and the merchants can do more business. If the city is healthy, people will live longer and they will not have to pay such large bills for doctors and nurses. The streets when well lighted at night become safer to walk and drive on. The schools enable thousands of children to become more intelligent and skilful, and able to earn better wages as soon as they go to work.

There is a farmer who spends money enough to have the best tools and wagons and mowing or reaping machines, and good horses and the best kind of cows. He keeps his barns in repair and feeds his cattle generously; and he takes care of his machines and tools. Altogether he spends a great deal of money upon his farm, and he employs men to help him.

Alongside of this farmer is another who fears to spend anything; he is a miser. He has no tools but old and broken ones; he has no machinery to help

do his work ; he will not pay workmen to help him.
He will not buy the best cows or horses. The rain
leaks through the roof of his barn. His cattle suffer
with the cold.

Which of these men, do you think, will make the
most money out of his farm: the one who spends
as little as he can ; or the first, who lays out money
to keep everything in good working order?

A city is somewhat like a great farm. The city is
not poorer, but richer, when its people spend money
to keep it in excellent condition. Men hear about
such a city, and they come to live in it, and to edu-
cate their children there. Strangers come to visit it,
and to buy goods and to spend money there in many
ways. Its people, being intelligent, do better work
and get better pay on account of their schools and
public libraries. As Black Beauty, the horse, in the
story, worked better for being comfortable and happy,
so the people are more prosperous for being well
and happy, for having parks and public gardens and
playgrounds.

CHAPTER XVIII.

THE TAXES, OR SHARING AND SHARING ALIKE.

WE generally use the word *share* when something good is to be divided among a number of persons. We use the same word also when something is to be done. We say that each one ought to do his fair share of the work, or to pay his share of the cost, just as each expects to enjoy his share of the pleasure or the profit that comes from the work.

Every one is eager to have his share of the enjoyment of what the city offers, of the parks and the library and the highways; every one wants to have a full share of the public money laid out in his own part of the city; every one desires a good sidewalk in front of his own house. But what shall we say about the work and the cost that must go to make a fine city? Is every one eager to do his fair share of this work, or to contribute his part of the cost? Let us see whether any honest man can want to get his fair share, and not be willing to do his fair share too.

We talk about the "public money." But where does the public money come from? It comes from the pockets of the people. In other words, it comes from the work, the earnings, the wages, the salaries, the income of all the people. This money that the people have to pay is called a *tax*. But this tax is not the same amount of money for every one. Would it be fair or just if a poor man in a little house paid as much as a rich man in a big house? Every one, therefore, must pay taxes according to the amount of property that he owns. If he has lands and houses and a large income, and spends much upon himself every year, he ought to pay also largely for the good of the city. You would not think any man would be so mean as to wish to get off with paying a cent less than his share!

Suppose a party of boys were working hard with spades and wheelbarrows to lay out and level a tennis-court. You would not think that the little boys ought to do as much work and wheel as much earth as the large and strong fellows. Suppose a big boy could do as much in an hour as a smaller boy in the whole afternoon; you would not think that the big boy would wish to quit work at the end of the hour and leave the little one to toil all day. Least of all would you think that any boy would be so mean as to get rid of his own share of work and so make the others do his work for him. What boy would have the face to come and use the tennis-court, after having shirked his work and run away while the others were digging and wheeling earth? We say, let us all "share and share alike," in the fun and in the work too.

So we say of our taxes. Suppose we divide all the cost of our town or city, and find that the average tax, if every one could pay the same amount, would be, say fifty dollars for every family. Indeed, in some cities it would be more than one hundred dollars for every family. Perhaps your teacher or your father can find out how much the average tax for every family is in your own town or city.

Now in some families the children would not have enough to eat if the father had to pay as much as fifty dollars a year for his tax to the city. Even if a man earned two dollars every day, you see that it would take twenty-five days, or about a month, to earn the amount of his tax.

How large a tax do you think that a rich man, who spends twenty or more dollars a day on his own living, ought to pay in order to do his fair share of the city work along with his poor neighbor? If the poorer man pays fifty dollars, probably the other ought not to pay less than five hundred dollars. But if the poorer man's family would suffer in being obliged to pay fifty dollars, ought not the other to pay more than five hundred dollars in order to do his just part? In fact, do you not think that the richer man ought to prefer out of his abundance to do more than his part rather than less?

It is not always easy to know how much each citizen pays as his tax. There is a tax on every house and shop and piece of ground in town. If your father owns the house you live in, he must pay the tax directly, so many dollars a year, to the town or city treasurer. But suppose he hires the house of

some one else. The other man, the owner of the
house, then pays the tax, but is very apt to think
that the man who lives in the house ought to pay the
tax back to him. If he can he makes the rent of the
house high enough to cover his tax. Whoever pays
the rent, therefore, is likely every month to pay a
part of the tax. Thus poor men often pay more
taxes than they think.

Why cannot a city have property of its own, as a
rich man has, and so get money without taxing its
people? A few cities do have property from which
they make money. A city may own wharves and
rent them. The city may have buildings,—for instance, a market-house. The city of Philadelphia
once owned its gas works. Glasgow in Scotland, and
other cities, own street railways. But no city in the
world is rich enough to live without asking its people
to pay taxes.

What does a city do when once in a while it needs
a vast deal of money, for instance, to build a new
high school or city hall, or to lay out a new park?
It might raise a little higher tax that year, and pay
for its new building as fast as it is erected. In fact,
however, most cities borrow money for such great
pieces of work. There are rich men, or perhaps sav-
ings-banks, that are very willing to lend money to a
city. By and by the city must pay back every dollar
of the borrowed money. Very likely it will borrow
again in order to pay its debt as fast as it is due.
The debt of some cities is nearly as large as the

value of all their public property, parks and buildings and everything else.   The debt of the city of
Boston is about one hundred dollars for every man,
woman, and child in the city.

We think it is rather bad business for a man to be
in debt.   If he wishes to buy a new bicycle or his
wife wishes to paper her dining room, we think he
had better contrive to pay for this extra work out of
his salary or income.   The man who goes into debt
and borrows whenever he wants anything is likely to
become reckless and wasteful.   Neither, in the long
run, is he as well off, for he has to pay ever so much
interest, and his debts always stare him in the face.

Do you not think it would be better if our towns
and cities were more careful about borrowing money?
You know that whoever borrows money must each
year pay a certain sum as *interest*.   Cities and towns
must pay interest also.   Since they borrow great
amounts of money, they are obliged to pay large
sums, in the case of great cities, millions of dollars
every year.   The taxes are made larger in consequence.   The poor as well as the rich have to bear
this burden of expense for borrowed money.

If to-day Boston and Chicago and New York had
no interest money to pay, these cities could have all
the fine new school buildings they need, and public
music halls besides, without either borrowing money
or raising any more taxes.

There is an old saying that "the borrower is the
servant of the lender."   The people who pay interest

help support those who lend money. Do you suppose it is good for our country to have a great many
of its people always in debt, while others live by
lending their money instead of working? Ought not
every one in the land to be doing some useful work
for the sake of the rest?

CHAPTER XIX.

THE CITY BEAUTIFUL, OR WHAT WE WISH FOR OUR CITY.

LET us try to imagine now the best kind of city, such as we should like to live in. It will do no harm if we imagine a greater and more beautiful city than any which now exists in Europe or America. It will do no harm to wish for a city so fine that it will take more than a hundred years to bring it about. It is not necessary, therefore, that the children who help make this picture of a city shall all live now in any actual city. Some of them may live on farms in the country; some may always continue to live in the country. Nevertheless, they can help us to tell what kind of a city they would like now and then to visit.

In the first place, let us suppose that we are approaching our fine city on a railroad train or by the electric cars. What shall we see? Not, as we often see in approaching a city, wretched, ugly, tumble-down buildings and mean tenement houses, so that we wish to shut our eyes before the train arrives at the station, — but houses with little gardens about them, and flowers in their windows, and trees by the sides of the streets. Even the workshops and factories will have vines on their walls wherever vines will grow. The people of our city do not like to look upon ugly and ruinous things, or to let children grow up in narrow, dingy attics and cellars without light or air. Every family in the city has some comfortable space, and as fast as possible a house for itself. The poor, as well as the rich, therefore, live a little outside of the busy, crowded centre of the town, where the banks and stores are.

As we pass along, we see no glaring bills or posters painted or printed on the walls and fences to advertise all kinds of quack medicines and absurd shows. People have become tired of seeing every rock and field disfigured.

As soon as we arrive within the city and begin to walk about, we shall admire the cleanness of the streets. The people do not throw bits of paper and other dirty things into the gutters. No one ever spits upon the side-walks. The pavements are smooth, so that there is the least possible noise or jolting as you ride over them. No one upon the streets is smoking. People have made up their minds that it is a nuisance and bad manners to blow tobacco-smoke into other people's faces. They no more think of smoking on the crowded streets than of eating their lunches there.

You turn to ask your way of some one. Any one will be glad to stop and answer a stranger's questions. The people are busy, but they do not look

jaded and restless and anxious, as if they had not a
friend in the world.   On the contrary, they look
contented, happy, and friendly.

You wish to see some of the public buldings.   They
are the noblest buildings in the city.   They are

ASHLAND BOULEVARD, CHICAGO.

The doctors tell us that if we kept all our streets perfectly clean,
like this beautiful Chicago avenue, we should save the lives of
thousands of people every year, who now catch disease by breathing poisonous dust.

simple, but they are built upon honor so as to last for
centuries.   All the schoolhouses have ample playgrounds about them.   There are gymnasiums for both
boys and girls in every quarter of the city.   This

accounts for the handsome appearance and the erect bearing of the children whom you see going to and from school. There are baths, too, free to all the people. No boy or girl grows up without learning to swim. Even in the winter, the public baths are open just as in the summer.

We must visit the city hall, where the mayor's office is, and the treasurer's, and the rooms for the city council. All the business of the city is carried on here. The big building is not huddled away in a narrow street, and crowded upon by shops and stores. It occupies a great square, and has a garden about it.

We now go to the fire engine houses. There are powerful electric engines for putting out fires, but the men tell us that there are not many fires. People now build solid and fireproof houses and stores. No one is allowed to keep a great wooden fire-trap, full of danger to all the city.

We ask for the police stations and the jails. They are not on the main streets, and they are very plain buildings. It is the pride of the city that the policemen have to arrest but few people. Moreover, when any one is found who has so little regard for his neighbors as to steal goods and money, to assault another, or to be drunken and violent, he is sent away from the city altogether. The city has a reform school and farm away off in the country; no one can return from the reform school to the city to live, unless he is prepared to work for his living like a good and friendly citizen.

As we walk the streets we are surprised to see no liquor saloons. The people have decided that these saloons are a nuisance, so that no one now wants to see them open. They made people drunk and unhappy. If any one really needs wine or anything of that sort, there are public stores where such things can be bought. But no one can loaf about in these places. Neither is any one allowed to make any money by selling intoxicating drinks.

What do all the men do in our fine city, who used to spend their evenings in the liquor saloons? They must have some way of enjoying themselves. In every ward or district of the city there are ward buildings and halls, where at election times the citizens have their meetings or caucuses. These halls belong to the people, and they are kept clean and warm and light all the time. They have reading rooms where men can read and write if they wish. They contain branches of the public library, so that the people can get books near their homes. There are "smoking rooms" where men can talk with their friends. There are rooms for games, too, where no smoking is allowed, and where children can play within certain hours, when the older people are not using them.

In every one of these halls there is a refreshment room. The city health officers see that everything sold in it is excellent and wholesome, and the charges are low. There are other conveniences for the citizens and for strangers. The hall is used frequently for entertainments, and especially for concerts of music. These are often given by the city, which keeps a staff of public organists and other musicians, out of the money that once had to be spent for supporting idle and harmful people.

Throughout the city there are many beautiful churches. But no one asks whether they belong to the rich or the poor. For all use them alike. They welcome every one within their doors. No one is given a better seat because of the fine clothes that he wears. The people learn in their churches to be true, honorable, courteous, and gentle, as well as reverent and fearless. Any one would be ashamed to come away from his church and cheat or injure his neighbor. People differ in some things about their religion, but all agree in good-will toward one another. All hold the religion of "loving their neighbors as themselves."

Let us now take a carriage or an electric car and go through the magnificent driveways and parks. The whole city is dotted with these public grounds. No one has to go far to find an open breathing space. Wherever there is a fine view by the river side, or over the harbor, or upon a hilltop, the city has given its people an entrance to it. There are miles of walks by the water. We can also see the gardens around the hospitals for the sick, and about the public homes where old men and women who have no children of their own to live with, are kindly cared for.

We see men at work in various places in the pay

of the city.   No one is obliged to work more than eight hours a day at the most.   But all are doing the city work exactly as if it were their own.   Is it not really their own work?   Is it not also work for the sake of their own friends, neighbors, and fellow-citizens?   No one thinks of shirking or dawdling.   It is cheerful and happy work; the city furnishes the best tools, machines, and other helps.   The superintendents and overseers are as respectful to their men as if they were brothers.   No man who works for the city, so long as he is faithful, is in any more danger of losing his place than any faithful man in the service of a wise and good private employer.

Our beautiful city does much more for its people than cities did in old times.   Perhaps it runs the street-cars; it may supply pure milk to its people: the city can afford to do more than cities once did. It uses its money without waste or loss.   Its officers are honest, and are always looking after the public welfare.   Its people are happy and intelligent, and every one wishes to purchase goods of their excellent workmanship.   Trade and business are good.   Visitors are always coming to the city from all parts of the world.   The very best men and women choose this city to live in.   Let us all work and vote to help make a real city like this city of our dreams.   It is quite possible to do this.

CHAPTER XX.

A MODEL TOWN.

THE people who live in cities doubtless have much
to enjoy. There are all sorts of things to see in the
shop windows; new buildings are always being erected.
There are jostling crowds and fine carriages upon the
streets; the great thoroughfares at night are almost
as bright as day; there are lectures and concerts and
plays. A great deal of money is spent to make people comfortable and happy. But it is very doubtful
whether the city people are happier than the people
who live in the country.

Let us count up some of the good things that the
country people enjoy. They have the broad fields
and the orchards and woods, and maybe the ocean
and an ample view of the great sky over them. They
can roam about freely, and when the grass is mown
and the harvests are in, they can climb over the walls
and fences and go almost wherever they please, as if
all the land were their own. The city boys and girls
hardly ever see the cows that give them milk, or the
lambs at play, or the young colts frisking in their
pastures. The country children can make friends
and pets of all these creatures. They can hear the

birds singing, and learn the secret of where they make their nests. The boys can go fishing and bathing. In the great pine forests of the South the boys go sliding down the steep hillsides on the pine needles, smooth as ice. In the winter, in all the Northern country, there will often be jolly coasting, sleighing, and skating parties.

The country children see many interesting kinds of work going on. They can learn to harness and drive the horses, and to ride bareback or in the saddle. They can learn how to plant and sow and tend the growing corn, the peas and the beans and the turnips. City children often do not know the difference between one kind of plant and another, between spruce trees and pines, between maple trees and beeches. But the country children learn these things as easily as they breathe.

The country children see the blacksmith shoeing horses, or putting tires on the wagon-wheels. They can stand inside the door of the carpenter's shop, and perhaps help him about his work. They can watch the cream as it is being churned into butter, and see how cheese is made. In the country, people are not often obliged to put up notices as they do in the city, "No Admittance," or "Boys not wanted Here." If boys and girls are civil and do not stand in the way, they can look on and see how work is done. Indeed, they are often needed to help their fathers or mothers.

There are towns and country places where the people are exceedingly well off, perhaps better off than any city people are. You will find broad streets or roads arched over with noble trees. You will see great elms and oaks and chestnut trees that were planted long ago by the early settlers of the town. Excellent roads, as good as in any city, delightful to walk or ride over, traverse the country in every direction.

There will sometimes be several villages in the township, like tiny cities, with clean sidewalks and well lighted at night. The houses are well kept and tidy, and have nice gardens about them, with flowers and fruit trees. You will observe the schoolhouses, the town hall, and the public library. The city people have larger buildings, but none that are better. Neither do they have better teachers for their schools.

As you drive about the town, you will observe what good barns and stables the cattle and the horses live in. These country people want their animals to be as comfortable as they are themselves. Notice the walls and fences; see the farm tools and machinery; everything is orderly. There is a place for everything, and everything seems to be in its place. It is not thought quite decent in this town to have broken glass in a window, or to keep an unsightly woodpile in front of a house, or to leave the horse-rake in the field to rust.

Perhaps some one wants to know where the poor people live in this fine town. There are not any really poor people. Every one has his little home and a bit of ground. No one in town ever suffers for want of food. Every one can read and write. You will not find a single liquor saloon in the town. There are people who have grown up without ever having seen a drunken man.

Perhaps you will be on the main street in the village about nine o'clock in the morning. You may look up and see a great covered wagon, filled with children. They have come in from their homes, two, three, or four miles away, to attend school. The town pays for bringing them to school and taking them home every day. Once there were little schoolhouses, scattered over the town, in every district where children lived. Little children and grown boys and girls went to school together. But the school committee found that they could not provide good teachers for these small schools; neither could the same teacher give proper attention to young pupils just learning to read, and older pupils who wished to study algebra and Latin. The committee now bring all the school children in the town to a central school, and they place them in the classes where they each belong, some in primary classes, some in the grammar school, and others in the high school.

The model town is always looking after better ways of making its people happy. Perhaps the town needs to have a new supply of pure water, and the citizens agree or vote at town meeting to spend money for laying the pipes and pumping the

water. There will be lectures and entertainments in
the town hall on winter evenings. There will be
good and fast trains on the railroad to convey the
people who wish to visit the neighboring city. City
people will like to come out to spend their summer
in such a fine town, or even to live there all the year.

How is it that one town can be vastly better to live
in than another? It depends upon the character of
the citizens. In some towns the people have a great
deal of public spirit; that is, they are generous, en-
lightened, and civilized. They want the very best
things for themselves and their children, and their
neighbors also. Instead of being selfish and miserly,
they are willing to be taxed and to pay their money
for good schools, and good roads, and whatever the
whole town needs. The public-spirited citizen does
not say, "I have a good well and all the water I
want for myself; I do not wish to spend money
for getting water for other people." He asks whether
it will be for the good of the whole town to have a
public water-supply, and he votes accordingly.

The public-spirited citizen is not so mean as to say:
"The road in front of my house is good enough; I
do not wish to pay taxes to build a new road for the
people at the other end of this town." He asks
whether the new road is needed. Is it for the good
of the town? Is it not fair to give all the people the
benefit of good roads?

The public-spirited people go promptly to town
meeting, and plan together for the welfare of their

town. They will not choose dishonest selectmen or treasurers, but they seek the best men in the town for these offices. They do not ask whether the best man belongs to their party, or to their church, or whether he is a relative of their own. They only need to know that he is wise and faithful, and that he will fill the office for the good of the people. Then they proceed to elect him.

Perhaps you have seen a town where everything was slack and slovenly. The houses had no paint upon them; the barns were tumbling to ruin; the fences were down; old hats were thrust into the broken windows; there were liquor saloons in the village; you could see through the cracks in the walls of the mean little schoolhouses; no one ever wished to buy a farm in such a town. What was the trouble with the wretched little town. Was it because its people were poor? But what made and kept them poor? It was because the people lacked generous, public spirit. They were narrow-minded, mean, and selfish toward their own town. The truth is, you never can have a model town till its citizens learn to be generous, to work together, and to help one another in making their town comfortable, prosperous, and happy.

STATE CAPITOL, AUSTIN, TEXAS.

Texas has an area much larger than the Empire of Germany. What a great duty the men have who sit in its Capitol, and what a grand chance they have in making good laws for millions of people!

CHAPTER XXI.

OUR STATE AND OUR GOVERNOR.

You all know what the capital of your State is, and how far away it is from where you live. You know how your State is bounded and what other States are its neighbors. Perhaps you have been in the capital. The State House is there. It may not be the most beautiful public building in all the State, but it is very likely the largest and most costly. There are many handsome offices in it, and two chambers, or halls, where the men meet who make the laws for the people of the State. There is a room for the governor, and probably a fine library with many books.

We have seen how all the people of a town or city join or club together in managing their public business. They meet for themselves, or else choose some of their men to meet in their behalf, and they plan together for the interests of the people. They must all bear their part of the cost of taking care of their town or city.

Now in somewhat the same way all the towns and cities, or in some States the counties and the cities, join together and select men to do business for all the people of their State. It would never be possible to get all the hundreds of thousands, or even millions, of the people into one place. But every year, or every two years, they choose men, the senators from large districts of the State, and the representatives from the cities and towns or counties, to go to the capital and talk and vote in their name. Whatever the Senate and the House of Representatives agree to do, the people must accept, as if they had done it themselves. The two chambers, the Senate and the Representatives, make the Legislature.

Why should there be two bodies of men, instead of one, to do business for the people? We can only say that this is an old custom. Some think that it is a foolish custom; others say that two bodies of men who must agree about everything which they do, are likely to be more careful not to do foolish things. It does not really make much difference whether there

are two chambers or only one.   But it makes a great
deal of difference whether the people choose their
best men to go to the State House, or let ignorant,
selfish, and dishonest men go to represent them.

STATE CAPITOL, ALBANY, N.Y.

This is a splendid and costly building. But its walls tell a sad
story of the unfaithfulness of the people's servants and the waste of
the public money.

For there are always too many of the wrong kind of
men who wish to sit in the great arm-chairs in the
Senate chamber, or in the Assembly room in the
State House, to draw the pay for themselves and
to have a hand in appointing their own friends to

offices.   There have never as yet been enough men
who go to the State House for the good of the people,
and for that only.

As the city has a mayor, or head officer, so each
State has a governor.   He is the highest officer in
the State.   His duty is to be always looking out, not
for the interest of the town where he happens to live,
or the city where he owns a mill, but for all the towns
and cities and all the counties of the State.   He is
governor for the sake of the whole State.

Whenever the members of the Legislature meet in
the State House, the governor sends them a message
or letter to tell them what he thinks is needed for the
welfare of the State.   If the Legislature makes a bad
law or votes to waste the State money, the governor
must tell them what he thinks about it, and he must
ask them to vote upon it more carefully again.   The
rule is that the governor must sign with his own hand
every law that the Legislature makes.   If he thinks
any law bad for the people, it will take as many as
two-thirds of the senators and the representatives to
pass it against the veto of the governor.

It sometimes happens that the governor does not
like a bill or law well enough to sign it, but he does
not object to it enough to wish to veto it.   In this
case, after a certain number of days, it becomes law
without his signing it.

The members of the Legislature meet to talk and
plan and to vote.   After they get through with
making plans and laws for the good of the State,

they go to their own homes, where most of them
have business of their own.   There are regular officers or servants of the State, who give their whole
time to carrying out the votes or laws that the Legislature passes.   The governor appoints many of the
chiefs, or superintendents, of the work of the State.
In some States he appoints judges for the courts.

You can see what a wise and courageous man he
needs to be in order to secure first-rate officers to
serve the people.   He needs to know who the good
and honest men and women are in all parts of the
State.   Like the mayor of a city, he must be able to
say *No*, if ever the men of his party ask him to appoint an unfit man to serve the State.   What right
has he to put unfit men into office?   This would be as
bad as if a carpenter put rotten timber into a house.

The governor is chosen by all the people of the
State.   In other words, all the citizens are expected
to vote for a governor, and the man who receives
more votes than any one else is elected.   It is a great
honor which the people give to their governor in
choosing him to stand as their captain and defender.

What is the use of having a State government?
Why cannot the towns and cities make all their own
rules and laws and take care of all the public business?   In other words, what does the State do for its
people?

Suppose for a moment that every city or town had
its own set of laws.   Suppose that what was allowed
in your town was forbidden in the next town.   Sup-

pose also that every town had to keep a judge and a court-house and sheriffs, and a jail to put offenders in. How clumsy all this would be! Do you not see that it is necessary for the people in all the towns to do many things together, instead of doing them separately? Thus it is well to have one set of laws for the whole State, and a few courts rather than a court in every village.

What if the people of one town built a dam across a river and flooded the meadows in the towns higher up the river? What if the great city wished to build a reservoir and to take all the water of the ponds miles away in the country? There must be some order or authority in the State so that no town can do harm to the people of another town.

The State needs great highways to connect all parts of its country. Perhaps it needs canals and railroads. Who shall say where the canals must run? Who shall see that the railroads pay justly for taking people's land? Who shall decide whether it is wise to allow a new railroad to be built? The Legislature must guard the interests of the people in all such matters.

The governor and the Legislature have many poor and unfortunate persons to provide for. There are orphan children in the State; there are aged and helpless people; there are insane people who cannot take care of themselves; there are those who have broken the laws. Some of these unfortunate people are not citizens of any town. They have never earned their living anywhere.   The State must take care of them; it must build great homes or hospitals for them; or its officers must find kind friends who will adopt the orphan children.   The State must also see that all the towns have good schools.   What if any town

THE STATE HOUSE, SACRAMENTO, CALIFORNIA.

California was mostly a wilderness before 1850. See what a palace its people have built in which to carry on their business!

were so poor or so mean that it would not give its children a decent education?   These ignorant children would be dangerous, wherever they went to live in other towns.   The laws of the State therefore require every town to maintain schools.   If necessary, the rich towns must help the poor towns rather than let the children of the State suffer.

The work of the State costs a great deal of money. Where will this money come from? It must come from the people themselves. The State is only another name for the people. Every town (or county) and every city must contribute its part to the State treasury. The richer the town, the larger will its just share be toward paying the salaries of the servants of the State and doing the State work. But the city or town has no money to pay, except what comes from the labor and the property of the people. Their taxes support the State.

Would it not be a good plan if the State, that is, all the people, owned property such as lands and forests and mines, so as to get money without the need of taxes? In some countries, the State has property of its own. In some of our States, too, there are vast areas of public lands. In every State all the most beautiful places, such as Niagara Falls, the White Mountains, the Adirondacks, the beaches on the seashore, ought to be held by the State and kept open to the people forever.

We have said that all the people must pay their share of the taxes. But suppose that the people of some city, or those in one part of the State, were unwilling to pay. Would it be fair for a few people, or for one part of the State, to refuse to help in doing what the larger number of the people wished to do? What if every one refused to do his part whenever he chose not to help? Do you not see that this would be mean and selfish, as when spoiled children sulk and stop playing if they cannot have their own way? How can you expect the others to help you when your side has its innings, unless you will stand by and play when the other side is at the bat?

But what if the other party does what seems to us wrong? In this case we can talk with our neighbors and try to persuade them to change their minds. We can seek to elect the men who agree with us. We can try to alter a bad law and make a good one. Let us not forget that we sometimes make mistakes ourselves. We must be fair to the other party, and give them a chance to persuade us. Is there any one in the world so wrong-headed and stupid as the person who never changes his mind?

What sort of State do you wish to live in? It is a State that has just laws for all, where no one can easily oppress or take advantage of another, where the same laws hold for the poor as for the rich, where strangers are safe and respected. It is a State whose schools are the best in the world, whose children are happy, where every one has a chance to make the most of himself. It is a State that takes the kindest care of all its unfortunate people, that tries to cure its sick, and to make good citizens even out of those who have done wrong. It is a State whose officers, from the governor down, are the real and faithful servants of the people.

CHAPTER XXII.

THE HEAD OF THE NATION.

THE capital of the United States is the city of Washington. Every one knows for what great and good man this city was named. Perhaps you, or some one of your friends, have visited the beautiful city on the banks of the Potomac River. You can tell how far away it is from where you live, and over what railroads you must ride in order to reach it.

What are the first objects that any one would see as he rode into Washington? One of them is the tall monument to the honor of "The father of his country." It is faced with white marble and is one of the tallest structures ever erected by man. It is not only very high, but beautiful also.

Another great building is the Capitol, or the State House of our Nation. It stands on a hill and has a grand dome, upon which is a cupola, to which one can climb and look out over the whole city, and to the distant mountains between which the Potomac flows. The Capitol contains many offices, and two halls, where men come together, chosen from every State of our Union, to consult for the welfare of all the people of the Nation. One hall is for the Senate.

Two senators come from each State, from the little States like Delaware, as well as from the great States like New York.

The other hall in the Capitol is for the House of Representatives. The great States send many representatives, as many as thirty or more. A little State may send only one man. You can easily find out how many representatives your own State sends. Perhaps you can tell who the representative is for your own district.

The Senate and the Representatives make the Congress of the United States. The business of the Congress is to *think* for the people. As the City Council thinks for the city, and the Legislature thinks for the State, so the Congress thinks for the nation, that is, for all the people in all the States. What good and bright thinkers the members of our Congress ought to be, in order to think well for the interests of more than seventy millions of people. Indeed, they have to think about people over the sea also; for the things which our Congress does, whether right or wrong, whether wise or foolish, are likely to help or to hurt all the people in the world. Thus, if the United States shuts its doors against the people who wish to come here from Italy, or from Germany, those countries will become crowded and perhaps uncomfortable. Or, if the United States lays a tax upon the silks, or the woollen cloths, that come from France and England, it may be that the French and English workmen will get less pay in consequence of our tax.

The members of our Congress must not only think for us, but they are chosen to make laws for the whole nation, as each Legislature makes laws for the people of its State. Whatever they agree to, or vote for, or rather whatever the larger number of them agree to in our behalf, we must all likewise agree to. We must obey their laws and we must pay our money, as they say, to help bear the cost of our government.

See what a number of sets of rules, or laws, the people must obey. They must keep the town, or city (or county) rules. They must heed the State laws, and they must also observe the national laws. But, as we have seen, these various laws are not meant to burden us. They are really intended for our convenience and benefit, like the rules of a school, or a store. They are for the sake of order and justice.

There are some things that not even the people of a great State like Texas or Illinois, can do well without the help of all the other States. Think of the great railroads and express companies with lines that run across the continent. Think of the great mills and shops that send their goods over all the country. Think of the men who travel from one State to another as agents to sell the merchants' wares. There must be laws to govern and to assist the men and the companies who go for their business from one State into the other States. No great company must be allowed to do injustice anywhere; no State must pass laws to hurt the people of another State.

WASHINGTON MONUMENT.

This is another of the wonders of the New World. Think of the highest building you know, and find out how many times higher this great shaft is — 555 feet high! All the States contributed stones to build into the walls. You can go to the top of it.

The people in Maine or Alabama who buy goods from the New York merchants must pay for what they buy as fairly as if they lived in New York. There must be laws also for the business of the post-offices through all the country, and for many other affairs which concern every man, woman, and child in the United States.

The nation has a good deal of land that belongs to us all, especially in the great Western territories and in Alaska. There are Indians who must be justly treated. The settlers must not rob them, and the Indians must not steal the settlers' horses.

Our nation has neighbors, we mean the other nations, Canada to the north of us, and Mexico and the Republics of South America, and the peoples over the Atlantic and across the Pacific Ocean. Congress must pass laws and make treaties, so that we shall treat each nation justly, and so that we shall also be justly treated.

You see what a great deal of puzzling business Congress has to think about. It is no wonder that it has built, at the expense of the nation, a grand library, close to the Capitol, filled with books on every subject. Whenever a member of Congress or of one of its committees needs to know about any matter of history, or geography, or about the laws of nations, here are the books to consult which give the needful information. The library may also be visited by the people, and by strangers in Washington.

There is a famous room in the Capitol where you

may see the greatest court of justice in the world. The nine members of this court are dressed in black silk robes. It is the Supreme Court of the United States. Here lawyers come from every State of our Union to bring difficult cases. Sometimes a State has passed laws that seem unjust to the citizens of

THE WHITE HOUSE.

From the windows of the marble house where the President lives one can look down Pennsylvania Avenue to the Capitol. Can you think of any children who lived in the White House while their father was President ?

another State. Sometimes there is a question about a new invention ; and two or three men each think that they ought to have the patent right for it. Sometimes Congress has levied a tax which business men do not think is just. When the Supreme Court makes a decision even Congress must give way. What if one of these judges were not perfectly honest and fearless? The rights and liberties of all of us would be endangered.

Who has not heard of the White House in Washington? Every visitor goes to see it. The President of the United States lives in this house; it is our national palace. As the Congress is the head of the nation to think and make laws for us; as the Supreme Court is the head of the nation to decide knotty questions; so the President is the head of the nation to act for us, and to see that the people's laws are carried out. A governor is chosen by all the people of a State to do the people's will; so the President is the choice of the people of all the States. As the mayor is the head servant of a city, so the President is the head servant of the nation. The best teacher who ever lived said that the greatest man in the world was the one who served most. Our President is thus chosen to serve and help, not himself, but our millions of people.

Our President could not begin to do his duty for the people without aid. He chooses a *Cabinet*, or council, of men to help him. These are his Secretaries, or advisers. The most important of these advisers is the Secretary of State. The famous Daniel Webster once held this office. Perhaps some one from your State has held the same place. This Secretary ought to be as wise as the President. He must advise the President about foreign affairs, concerning many different nations. He must not only be perfectly

fair, but he must be courteous and friendly. He
meets the ambassadors and ministers, that is, the
agents, whom other governments send to Washington. Suppose he could not keep his temper,
but insulted these foreign gentlemen; or suppose
he wrote disrespectful letters to the great governments in St. Petersburg or Berlin; he might involve
the nation in war. At the same time the Secretary

SMITHSONIAN INSTITUTE, WASHINGTON, D.C.

A rich Englishman, named Smithson, left his fortune to our
government to be used for the increase of knowledge among men.
Every one who visits Washington should see the wonderful curiosi-
ties that are collected in this building.

of State must be brave and patriotic. His place is
too high and responsible for any mean or selfish
man, who wishes merely to draw the salary or have
the honor of the office.

Next to the Secretary of State comes the Secretary
of the Treasury. He is really the head treasurer of

the vast moneys of the nation. He must know all about business; he must be able to advise as to the fairest methods of raising money for the government; he must be honest and accurate beyond suspicion; he must be fearless to tell the President, or the members of Congress, exactly what he thinks for the public welfare.

There is a Secretary of War, who looks after the business of the army, and a Secretary of the Navy who must see that the battle-ships are kept in order. Another of the President's advisers has the care of all the lands of the nation, and must guard the interests of the Indian tribes. He is called the Secretary of the Interior. Another is the President's adviser about matters of law; he is the Attorney-General. Another is at the head of the post-offices of the country; he is the Postmaster-General. Another must keep informed about all matters that concern the farmers. A large part of the wealth of the nation springs from the soil. What if some dangerous blight threatened the wheat? Or some foreign pest menaced the lives of the cattle? The Secretary of Agriculture, with the help of his agents, must be on guard to save the nation from the perils of insects, and from the diseases of plants. He must publish reports and pamphlets, so that the farmers may know how to raise larger and better crops and thus make our country richer.

The President, with the help of his advisers, or Cabinet, must not only do what Congress bids, but he must help the Congress to see what is for the welfare of the nation. A Congressman is too likely to ask, " What is for the good of my State, or of the people of the district that elected me?" The President takes a broad view of public business. He ought to be watching for the good of all the people. He is like a man on a tower, who sees farther than the man on the ground below.

The Representatives serve for two years and may then be reëlected. The Senators serve for terms of six years. The President serves for four years. A Vice-President also is chosen for four years. He presides over the Senate, and succeeds the President in case the latter dies before he finishes his term. Sometimes the President is liked so well that he is chosen a second time. Perhaps you can name the Presidents, beginning with Washington, to whom our people have done the honor of reëlecting them.

CHAPTER XXIII.

THE ARMY AND NAVY.

EVERY one has heard of the great battle-ships, such as the *Oregon* and the *New York*, the *Iowa* and the *Texas*. Many of our boys probably know how many ships and torpedo-boats the President and his Secretary of the Navy can command. There are stations, or navy yards, in certain harbors where these ships are fitted out, and where sailors are enlisted for them. Thousands of trained men are needed to man the ships and to fire the great ·guns. Engineers and stokers serve the engines. Hundreds of skilled officers must be highly educated to manage the government vessels. You have perhaps heard of the great school at Annapolis in Maryland, where the nation pays for training boys to be brave and skilful officers for the ships.

Upon hills or points of land near the harbors of the great cities one will see strong forts and batteries with gigantic guns. One of the greatest forts is called Fortress Monroe, after one of our Presidents. It is in the State of Virginia, and close to the mouth of Chesapeake Bay. Companies of soldiers of the national army live in barracks or rows of little houses in this fort.   There are soldiers likewise always ready to march, in forts in New York harbor and other places.   There are soldiers at various forts in the Territories where the wild Indians live.   American soldiers have even been required to go to distant shores, as to Cuba and Manila.

A BATTLE-SHIP.

Is it not a pity that such a magnificent and powerful ship should ever be doomed to be battered to pieces by shot, or blown up, or sunk in the sea?

Part of our army is made up of men who ride on horseback.   They are called the cavalry.   The infantry march on foot and carry rifles.   The artillery manage great guns mounted on wheels, and fire terrible volleys of shot and shell.   The President is the commander-in-chief of all the forces. Many generals, colonels, and other officers assist him to carry out his commands. Quartermasters supply the army with food and clothing. Physicians and surgeons accompany the soldiers to care for the sick and the wounded.

THE BARRACKS, WEST POINT, N.Y.

Our government has a great school at West Point on the Hudson River. Here a number of boys from every State are trained to become officers of the Army. General Grant was educated here. The course of training is very severe.

The regular army is not all the force that the President has at his command. In every State there are companies and regiments of militia, under the com-

mand of the governor of the State. Some of the
boys perhaps know men who are in the militia.
Every year these militia soldiers meet on certain
days to train or drill. They can be called out if
necessary to help the police. If there is danger to the
country and the President wants men, the governors
of the States must see to it that the militia answers
his call. In fact, if the President calls for men to
defend the country, every able-bodied man must be
ready, if need comes, to obey and serve as a soldier.

Great sums of money are spent every year to pay
the wages of soldiers and sailors and the salaries of
their officers; millions of dollars must go to buy ships
and guns and all kinds of supplies. When the men
are disabled in the service of the country it is the
custom to pay pensions, so that they and their families may not suffer want. Altogether the business of
the army and the navy, even in times of peace, if we
count the expense of the pensions, costs more than
all the schools and colleges in the land.

Why is it necessary for the American people to
have an army and a navy, and to stand ready to
fight? Why should we ever fire murderous guns and
try to kill people? Why are not fighting and killing
and war always wrong?

It is hard to answer these questions. One way to
answer them is this: The world was once filled with
savage men; they had never learned the laws of
kindness and mercy; they were cruel to their animals
and to their own children; they were afraid and sus-

SOLDIERS.

Soldiers look fine as one sees them parading our streets with joyous music. But how do we feel when soldiers have to maim and kill other men or to be maimed or killed themselves!

picious of strangers and foreigners. Many a time in these wild old times roving tribes of warriors would come over the lands, spoiling the corn-fields, burning the farmers' houses and barns, and carrying away boys and girls to be slaves. Our own forefathers long ago were just such wild, cruel people. Perhaps they did not know better. They had no humane religion to tell them that all men were their brothers. Few, if any of them, could read and write. The American Indians, when the first settlers came to America, were such wild and ignorant people. Their roving tribes had been fighting each other for hundreds of years. You see now that war was the state in which barbarous men lived. Sometimes they fought to plunder others; sometimes they fought to defend themselves from oppression.

Suppose now that all nations had ceased to be savage and cruel. Suppose that all nations had learned our American ideas of kindness and fair play and friendliness. Suppose that all religions bade men treat each other like brothers and live by the Golden Rule. Suppose that all nations had schools and kindergartens like ours in America, and every one could learn to read good books and noble poetry. In this case no nation would need to tax its people and to spend its millions of money upon soldiers and battle-ships. Indeed, we could have the extra money to spend in making better schools. We might use the thousands of men who are soldiers to build more comfortable houses for the poor to live in. No one would need to work so hard as many work now, if all the soldiers in the world could come home and help their neighbors at their work. Wouldn't it be fine if men were nowhere ordered to shoot and kill other men?

The trouble now is that many people in the world have not yet given up being savage and brutish. We have seen that there are people even in America who are mean and stingy and selfish; there are those who get drunk and lose their wits; there are some who are still cruel to animals and to children; and there are a few who will steal and do murder. Therefore we must have policemen and jails. A policeman must knock a brutal man down if necessary, rather than let him hurt a little child.

Well! There are tribes and nations in the world that are hundreds of years behind the times; they are not half civilized. We in America have learned to be intelligent, and not to fear hard work, and to help one another. But there are millions of people who think that the chief business of life is to fight, like brutes. Sometimes these unfortunate people have been badly treated and enslaved, and they have reason to distrust their fellows. Thus bad white men have often cheated the American Indians, and have sold whiskey to them and stolen their lands. Some of the Indians have come to hate white men, because some of our own people have behaved so badly to them.

What shall a people do who dislike the business

of killing men, but who are surrounded by savage
nations, or pirate nations, or bullying nations? Suppose the nation has wild and ignorant people, as we
have, within its own borders? The President and the
Congress cannot sit down and let our settlers be

U.S. TRAINING SHIP "ENTERPRISE" IN DRY DOCK AT NAVY
YARD, CHARLESTOWN, MASS.

The government takes a number of boys, and makes a ship into
a schoolhouse for them, and trains them to be able and skilful sea-
men.

butchered and their cattle and children carried off.
The government cannot let some selfish power over
the seas take our merchant ships and throw American

sailors into prison. Our government cannot run the
risk of letting some mad king pick a quarrel with us
and send a fleet of ships to seize our cities. Our government must defend our homes against the half-civil-
ized people in the world who have not learned yet to
do justly and kindly. If there are foolish nations
that are ready to fight and kill, we must have soldiers
and sailors to guard our shores against them. We
therefore say to our President and Congress: "Try
hard not to have war with our neighbors, the other
nations. Be just and generous to them." But we
also say: "Let no robbers break through the doors
of the nation to injure the people."

How large should our armies be? How many ships
should we have? Ought we to keep as many soldiers
as Russia or as many war-ships as England? No!
We do not wish to be a fighting nation, but a civilized
nation. All our greatest generals have hated war.
War does not fit American ideas. A savage goes
about armed with clubs and knives, but the more
civilized a man is the less use he has for weapons.
The savage is afraid; the civilized man is not afraid.
So with nations. The wild and thieving nation is
really afraid. The upright and friendly nation has
no cause for fear. Thus, the more civilized and the
better educated a nation is, the smaller the army and
navy that it needs.

Indeed, if our men always behaved justly and
kindly to the Indians and to the people over the
sea, it is quite possible that we should never need

OUR SAILORS.

War is terrible waste. When the great guns are fired, far the
larger part of all the shot and shell never hit the mark. These
men are trying to aim and fire accurately.

any army or navy. There is no defence in the world so mighty as justice and friendliness are. What man needs to carry pistols when he travels? The burglar or the coward is more likely to carry them than the brave and honest man is. So the nation that does justice has least need to fear war.

Is it ever right to hate the savage and brutal nations, the Indians on our border, the Turks over the seas? No, we do not really want to hate them. Even the soldiers who fight against them do not need to hate them. Hate does not make men brave. We are rather sorry for the savage people. They have not had the good chance that we have. If they had had our American opportunity to learn, they might be men whom we should like. We do not wish to hurt and maim and kill human beings, but we want to help make men of them if possible. We do not keep our army and navy for the sake of war, but to prevent war, and, as General Grant said, to "have peace."

CHAPTER XXIV.

THE ARMY OF PEACE.

As a stranger walks or rides about the streets of the city of Washington, he will be shown immense buildings, filled with offices. These great buildings belong to the government. A little army of people are at work in them daily. There is the Treasury Building, with hundreds of clerks, who attend to the money business of the government. Other officers and clerks in the great cities help in collecting and paying out the money. In many towns upon the coast and along the borders of Canada and Mexico there are custom-houses, where men, under the direction of the Secretary of the Treasury, collect money or taxes.

A large company of men and women, even in times of peace, serve in the Army and Navy building; they keep the records and accounts. You can find there lists of the names of all our soldiers and sailors. In another building are the lists and accounts of the thousands of men and women and orphan children, scattered over the land, who receive pensions, or payments of money from our government; for the nation is unwilling to let any family suffer which has given a soldier for the service of the country. The Pension Office in Washington, with its branch offices in different parts of the country, requires a considerable force of helpers to do the work and to see that all the pensions are promptly paid.

ENTRANCE TO THE NAVY YARD, CHARLESTOWN (BOSTON), MASS.

Our government has several large ship yards, with wharves and dry docks and rope-walks and repairing shops. Sometimes the government has built its own ships. Visitors are commonly permitted to look about the Navy Yards.

One of the most interesting places to see in Washington is the Patent Office. Whoever is bright enough to invent an ingenious contrivance, from a new kind of water-wheel to a flying machine, may send to this office and have his invention recorded in his name. Then no one can use or sell this invention without the permission of the inventor. You may see at the Patent Office a model of almost every invention that has been made in the last hundred years. A company of clerks are on service all the time to take care of these models and plans, and to record new inventions as fast as they come.

We have spoken of the Supreme Court of the United States. You must not think that all the business of justice for the nation is done by the men who sit in this grand room at the Capitol. The Supreme Court attends to none but important questions. In every part of the United States there are courts and judges and lawyers and a force of assistants in the service of our government.

LETTER CARRIER.

Are there letter carriers where you live? Would you like to have carriers bring the letters throughout all the country? If so, you must let your representative in Congress know what you want. Perhaps he will see how to bring this about.

What do you suppose is the largest business of our government? It is the Post-office. It employs scores of thousands of men. It has one of the greatest of the buildings in Washington. It has an office in every little village. Its carriers in their uniform

ELECTRIC MAIL CARS.

In a great city the mails must be carried to and from the railroad stations, and also to and from the branch post-offices in all parts of the city. They used to carry the mails in wagons. Now the electric roads carry little postal cars, in which men can sort the mail as they go.

are on the streets of every city. Yes! The Post-master-General may be said to command a great

STEAM RAILWAY MAIL CAR.

We have post-offices on wheels. They run on the railroads from city to city. They have men to sort the mails day and night, so as to lose no time in delivering the letters as soon as they arrive.

army.   All these serve for the convenience and comfort of the people.   It is their duty to see that letters,
papers, books, and all sorts of things trusted to the
mails, shall go as fast and as promptly as possible.
Sometimes they go on railroads, sometimes by
steamers, often on stage-coaches, sometimes on horseback.   The Post-office sends our letters for us, not
only through our own country from Eastport in
Maine to Portland in Oregon; it undertakes to carry
the mail over the world; it has its treaties with other
governments; it really binds the world together.

Your friend may be travelling in Egypt; or he
may be a sailor at Hong Kong.   Our government, or
"Uncle Sam," as we sometimes call it, only asks us
to put one of his little stamps upon our letter, and
presently fast steamships are passing it on around
the world till it finds our friend.   Perhaps men of a
dozen different nations, or twenty different languages,
help the letter along.   The whole world takes hold,
like our nation, in supporting the Post-office.

Who has never seen a lighthouse?   If you visit
the seashore, if you go down the harbor of any city
on the coast, if you sail a few hours along the shore
on the ocean, or on the Great Lakes, if you travel
down the Mississippi River, — there is no place
where steamers go, or vessels sail at night, where you
do not see the lighthouses shining.   They are on
hills and headlands; they are on little islands and on
bare rocks; sometimes they are ships moored fast by
heavy anchors, near dangerous shoals.   Our govern-

ment builds the lighthouses and commands men to keep the lights always burning. In the darkest

MINOT'S LEDGE LIGHT, OFF COHASSET, MASS.
This tall, stone lighthouse stands on a dangerous ledge and warns the ships to keep off, and shows them the way to Boston harbor.

night, when the storm lowers over the sea, the faithful men must watch and tend the lamps, and if the fog sweeps in, they must sound the fog-horn, perhaps for days at a time.

The lighthouses are not for our own sailors and ships alone; they are for the English and Italian and Spanish and German sailors, as well. We wish no poor mariners to be wrecked on our reefs; we wish to give our lights for the help of all who sail the sea.

What we do for others all the nations do for us. You will sail along the English coast and every cape

U.S. NAVAL OBSERVATORY, GEORGETOWN, D.C.

How does any one know exactly what time it is? By the clock or by watches. But who can set the clocks and watches, so that they will tell the truth? The skilful men in the observatories tell us every day, by watching the sun, precisely when it is noon. They tell us also about the sunrise and the moon-rise and the tides, and help make our almanacs.

sends out its friendly light. You will sail down into the Mediterranean Sea, and the mountainous coast of Spain or Italy will show you your way from light to light. All the world is becoming one family of nations with their common system of lighthouses.

The government does more for the sailors than to light the shores for their ships.   On every perilous point on the coast where ships sometimes go to wreck, you will see the life-saving stations, each with its little company of men, and its stanch boats ready to be launched at a moment's notice.   There men patrol and watch the shore for many miles.   They take turns in looking out upon the sea at night.   Sometimes they send up rockets to warn the ships not to come too near the rocks.   No soldiers are braver than these men must be.   In terrible winter storms, or when the tornado comes, they must risk their own lives to save the lives of others.   They never stop to ask whether the people in danger are their own friends, or utter strangers.   It is their duty to save the lives of foreign men just as if they were Americans.

It would take a long time to tell of all the kinds of work in which our government must employ its servants.   Men are always at work in the navy yards, keeping the ships in repair.   Men are on duty among Indian tribes, some to teach in their schools, and others to show the Indians how to farm their lands.   Chemists are at work for the government, making experiments about soils and plants.   They publish to the world what they find out.   A board of health watches against disease, and sends its doctors to examine ships coming to our ports from foreign lands.

Altogether we have likened the thousands of men

and women who serve our government to an army of soldiers. But it is an army of peace and not of war. It is not to frighten men, but to help and benefit them. It is not for the good of Americans alone, but for the good of all people.

What kind of a man do we need for a soldier? He must be brave and obedient; he must not serve for pay, or for a pension, or to get honor for himself, or in order to be promoted to a higher office. He must serve, as Washington and Grant served, simply for the sake of helping his country. They were not soldiers in order to get their living out of the country, but because the country needed them. They were soldiers for the sake of the welfare of the people.

The country needs the same kind of men for its army of peace. It wants obedient and faithful men to keep its accounts and to carry its mails. It wants kind and courteous men in its offices, who will do their best for the convenience of its people. It wants fearless and upright judges who will do no wrong. It wants friendly men in the Indian agencies, to help the Indians to become civilized. It wants men of courage in its lighthouses and at the life-saving stations. Our government cannot really bear to have mean and selfish men anywhere, but it needs men, as good as the very best soldiers, who are in its service for the sake of their country.

What does a good soldier desire more than anything else? He desires that the cause of his country shall succeed.   What does every good American wish most of all?   He wishes that his work may make his country richer and happier.   He wishes, like Abraham Lincoln, to leave his country better and nobler for his having served her.

CHAPTER XXV.

SUMMARY: THE FLAG.

LET us use the wings of our imagination and take a journey all the way from Canada to the Gulf of Mexico, from the Atlantic ocean to Alaska. We shall see our flag floating over schoolhouses and government buildings, over post-offices and custom-houses, over forts and navy yards. We shall find it on all the holidays above many a house and store and shop. We shall see the little flags that friends on Memorial Day have placed on the graves of soldiers and sailors.

Let us now cross the seas, and we shall still find the flag in many a distant foreign harbor. It will be seen in the great cities of Europe and Asia, showing where American ambassadors and consuls and other agents of our government may be found by their countrymen. It will fly over grand hotels where American travellers are staying. It will be seen upon ships and steamers as men sail the distant seas. Wherever we see it a warm and friendly feeling thrills our hearts.

What does the flag with its bright colors mean, that millions of children should salute it in their schools, and that grown men should be willing to take off their hats in its presence?

OUR FLAG.

How many different flags of the nations do you know? Is there any flag more beautiful than ours? What three flags do you like best?

The flag means the union of all our people throughout all our States and Territories. Whereas men in

different nations once feared and fought each other,
we now in America trust and help one another.   The
men of the South and the men of the North, the men
of the East and the men of the West, all fly the same
flag.   It is a sign that we are one people.

What does the flag tell us as often as we see it?
It tells us that no one in America is alone or friend-
less.   There is a mighty government with its laws
and its officers, that will not let any one be oppressed.
Once men could make slaves of their fellows.   Nowhere to-day under our flag can any man be enslaved.
We are all pledged to give every one in the land
justice and equal liberty.   We are pledged to give all
children a chance to be educated.   The flag is the
sign of our pledge to befriend one another.

What can the flag do for us, if we journey abroad
and visit foreign lands?   It tells us that our government will watch over our safety.   We have treaties
with other peoples promising us that their laws and
courts and police and soldiers will protect us equally
with their own people.   Once strangers were liable
to abuse wherever they travelled.   Now, wherever our
flag goes, it is a sign that our government will never
forget us.   The lonely or sick American sailor,
stranded in Liverpool or Marseilles or Algiers, can
find the American consul and get help to return to
his home.   Where the flag flies abroad, American
women or children can get friendly advice.

The flag is not merely a sign that the government
will help and protect us at home and abroad.   It is

also a call and a command to every one of us to stand by the government. Suppose every citizen wanted the help of the government for himself. Suppose all the people expected the government to provide for them. This would be as if every one in a house expected to be waited upon by the others. Who would do the work of the house, if every one thought only of what the others ought to do for him?

The truth is, the government depends upon every one of us. The flag tells us not of a pledge that some one else has made, but a pledge that we have made ourselves. When we look at the flag, we promise anew that we will stand by the common country; we will try to be true and faithful citizens. We promise to do our work so well as to

COLONIAL FLAG, 1776.
We have as many stripes here as there were colonies. How many stars have we now in our flag?

make the whole country richer and happier; we promise to live such useful lives that the next generation of children will have a nobler country to live in than we have had. We scorn, when we see the flag, to be idle and mean, or false and dishonest. We devote ourselves to America to make it the happiest land that the sun ever shone on.

The flag tells us one other message. It has been carried over fields of battle. Men have shouted " Victory " under it. But it is not a flag of war.

It is a flag of peace. It does not mean hate to any other people. It is a sign of brotherhood and good-will to all nations. Americans purpose to conquer by kindness, by justice, by simple truthfulness. Good Americans are pledged to make the world more prosperous, happier and better. We all say therefore, in the good poet Longfellow's lines, of the noble Union over which our flag flies : —

> Sail on, O Ship of State !
> Sail on, O Union, strong and great !
> Humanity with all its fears,
> With all the hopes of future years,
> Is hanging breathless on thy fate !
>
> Our hearts, our hopes, are all with thee, —
> Our hearts, our hopes, our prayers, our tears,
> Our faith triumphant o'er our fears,
> Are all with thee, — are all with thee !

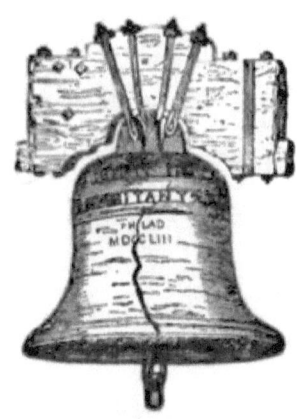

LIBERTY BELL.

ADVERTISEMENTS

Elementary English.

Badlam's Suggestive Lessons in Language **and Reading.** A manual for primary teachers. Plain and practical. $1.50.

Badlam's Suggestive Lessons in Language. Being Part I and Appendix of Suggestive Lessons in Language and Reading. 50 cts.

Benson's Practical Speller. Contains nearly 13,000 words. Part I, 261 Lessons, 18 cts.; Part II, 270 Lessons, 18 cts. Parts I and II bound together, 25 cts.

Benson and Glenn's Speller and Definer. Seven hundred spelling and defining lists. 40 cts.

Branson's Methods in Reading. With a chapter on spelling. 15 cts.

Buckbee's Primary Word Book. Embraces thorough drills in articulation and in the primary difficulties of spelling and sound. 25 cts.

Fuller's Phonetic Drill Charts. Exercises in elementary sounds. Per set (3 charts) 10 cents.

Hall's How to Teach Reading. Treats the important question: what children should and should not read. Paper. 25 cts.

Hyde's Lessons in English, Book I. For the lower grades. Contains exercises for reproduction, picture lessons, letter writing, *uses* of parts of speech, etc. 35 cts.

Hyde's Lessons in English, **Book II.** For Grammar schools. Has enough technical grammar for correct use of language. 50 cts.

Hyde's Lessons in English, Book II **with Supplement.** Has, in addition to the above, 118 pages of technical grammar. 60 cts. Supplement bound alone, 30 cts.

Hyde's Practical English Grammar. For advanced classes in grammar schools and for high schools. 50 cts.

Hyde's Derivation of Words. With exercises on prefixes, suffixes, and stems. 10 cts.

Mathews's Outline of English Grammar, with Selections for Practice. The application of principles is **made** through composition of original sentences. 70 cts.

Penniman's Common Words Difficult to Spell. Graded list of 3500 common words. 20 cts.

Penniman's Prose Dictation Exercises. For drill in spelling, punctuation and use of capitals. 25 cts.

Phillips's History and Literature **in Grammar Grades.** An essay showing the intimate relation of the two subjects. 15 cts.

Sever's Progressive Speller. Gives spelling, pronunciation, definition, and use of words. Vertical script is given for script lessons. 25 cts.

Smith's Studies in **Nature, and Language Lessons.** A combination of object lessons with language work. 50 cts. Part I bound separately, 25 cts.

Spalding's Problem of **Elementary Composition.** Practical suggestions for work in grammar grades. 40 cts.

See also our lists of books in Higher English, English Classics,
Supplementary Reading, and English Literature.

D. C. HEATH & CO., Publishers, Boston, New York, Chicago

Supplementary Reading

A Classified List for all Grades

GRADE I. Bass's The Beginner's Reader 25
    Badlam's Primer 25
    Fuller's Illustrated Primer 25
    Griel's Glimpses of Nature for Little Folks 30
    Heart of Oak Readers, Book I 25
GRADE II. Warren's From September to June with Nature . . .35
    Badlam's First Reader 30
    Bass's Stories of Plant Life 25
    Heart of Oak Readers, Book I 25
    Wright's Nature Readers, No. 1 25
GRADE III. Heart of Oak Readers, Book II 35
    Wright's Nature Readers, No. 2 35
    Miller's My Saturday Bird Class 25
    Firth's Stories of Old Greece 30
    Bass's Stories of Animal Life 35
    Spear's Leaves and Flowers 25
GRADE IV. Grinnell's Our Feathered Friends 30
    Heart of Oak Readers, Book III 45
    Kupfer's Stories of Long Ago 35
    Wright's Nature Readers, No. 3 50
GRADE V. Bull's Fridtjof Nansen 30
    Grinnell's Our Feathered Friends 30
    Heart of Oak Readers, Book III 45
    Wright's Nature Readers, No. 3 50
    Kupfer's Stories of Long Ago 35
GRADE VI. Starr's American Indians 45
    Bull's Fridtjof Nansen 30
    Heart of Oak Readers, Book IV 55
    Wright's Nature Readers, No. 4 60
GRADE VII. Starr's American Indians 45
    Penniman's School Poetry Book 30
    Heart of Oak Readers, Book IV 55
    Wright's Nature Readers, No. 4 60
    Dole's The American Citizen 90
GRADES VIII and IX. Heart of Oak Readers, Book V . . .65
    Heart of Oak Readers, Book VI 75
    Dole's The American Citizen 90
    Shaler's First Book in Geology (boards) 60
    Goldsmith's Vicar of Wakefield 50
    Addison's Sir Roger de Coverley 40

Descriptive circulars sent free on request.

D. C. HEATH & CO., Publishers, Boston, New York, Chicago

Heath's English Classics.

Addison's Sir Roger de Coverley Papers. Edited, with introduction and notes, by W. H. HUDSON, Professor of English Literature in the Leland Stanford Junior University. Cloth. 232 pages. Nine full-page illustrations and two maps. 40 cts.

Burke's Speech on Conciliation with America. With introduction and notes by ANDREW J. GEORGE, Master in the Newton (Mass.) High School. Boards. 119 pages. 25 cts.

Carlyle's Essay on Burns. Edited, with introduction and notes, by ANDREW J. GEORGE. Cloth. 159 pages. Illustrated. 30 cts.

Coleridge's Rime of the Ancient Mariner. Edited by ANDREW J. GEORGE. The text of 1817, together with facsimile of the original text of 1798. Cloth. 150 pages. Illustrated. 30 cts.

Cooper's Last of the Mohicans. Edited by J. G. WIGHT, Principal Girls' High School, New York City. With maps and illustrations. *In preparation.*

DeQuincey's Flight of a Tartar Tribe. Edited, with introduction and notes, by G. A. WAUCHOPE, Professor of English Literature in the University of South Carolina. Cloth. 112 pages. 30 cts.

Dryden's Palamon and Arcite. Edited, with notes and critical suggestions, by WILLIAM H. CRAWSHAW, Professor of English Literature in Colgate University. Cloth. 158 pages. Illustrated. 30 cts.

George Eliot's Silas Marner. Edited, with introduction and notes, by G. A. WAUCHOPE, Professor of English Literature in the University of South Carolina. Cloth. 000 pages. 00 cts.

Goldsmith's Vicar of Wakefield. With introduction and notes by WILLIAM HENRY HUDSON. Cloth. 300 pages. Seventeen full-page illustrations. 50 cts.

Macaulay's Essay on Milton. Edited by ALBERT PERRY WALKER, editor of Milton's "Paradise Lost," Master in the English High School, Boston. *Ready soon.*

Macaulay's Essay on Addison. Edited by ALBERT PERRY WALKER. *Ready soon.*

Milton's Paradise Lost. Books I and II. With selections from the later books, with introduction, suggestions for study, and glossary by ALBERT PERRY WALKER. Cloth. 288 pages. Illustrated. 45 cts.

Milton's Minor Poems. Lycidas, Comus, L'Allegro, Il Penseroso, etc, edited, with introduction and suggestions for study, by ALBERT PERRY WALKER. Cloth. 000 pages. Illustrated. 00 cts.

Pope's Translation of the Iliad. Books I, VI, XXII, and XXIV. Edited, with introduction and notes, by PAUL SHOREY, Professor in the University of Chicago. *In preparation.*

Scott's Ivanhoe. *In preparation.*

Shakespeare's Macbeth. Edited by EDMUND K. CHAMBERS, lately of Corpus Christi College, Oxford. In the *Arden Shakespeare* series. Cloth. 188 pages. 40 cts.

Shakespeare's Merchant of Venice. Edited by H. L. WITHERS. In the *Arden Shakespeare* series. Cloth. 178 pages. 40 cts.

Tennyson's Enoch Arden and the two Locksley Halls. Edited, with introduction and notes, by CALVIN S. BROWN, Professor in the University of Colorado. Cloth. 168 pages. 35 cts.

Tennyson's The Princess. With introduction and notes by ANDREW J. GEORGE, Master in the Newton (Mass.) High School. Cloth. 236 pages. Illustrated. 40 cts.

Webster's First Bunker Hill Oration. With introduction and notes by ANDREW J. GEORGE. Boards. 55 pages. 20 cts.

See also our lists of books in English Literature and Higher English.

D.C. HEATH & CO., Publishers, Boston, New York, Chicago

Elementary Science.

Austin's Observation Blanks in Mineralogy. Detailed studies of 35 minerals. Boards. 88 pages. 30 cts.

Bailey's Grammar School Physics. A series of inductive lessons in the elements of the science. Illustrated. 60 cts.

Ballard's The World of Matter. A guide to the study of chemistry and mineralogy; adapted to the general reader, for use as a text-book or as a guide to the teacher in giving object-lessons. 264 pages. Illustrated. $1.00.

Clark's Practical Methods in Microscopy. Gives in detail descriptions of methods that will lead the careful worker to successful results. 233 pages. Illustrated. $1.60.

Clarke's Astronomical Lantern. Intended to familiarize students with the constellations by comparing them with fac-similes on the lantern face. With seventeen slides, giving twenty-two constellations. $4 50.

Clarke's How to find the Stars. Accompanies the above and helps to an acquaintance with the constellations. 47 pages. Paper. 15 cts.

Guides for Science Teaching. Teachers' aids in the instruction of Natural History classes in the lower grades.
- I. Hyatt's About Pebbles. 26 pages. Paper. 10 cts.
- II. Goodale's A Few Common Plants. 61 pages. Paper. 20 cts.
- III. Hyatt's Commercial and other Sponges. Illustrated. 43 pages. Paper. 20 cts.
- IV. Agassiz's First Lessons in Natural History. Illustrated. 64 pages. Paper. 25 cts.
- V. Hyatt's Corals and Echinoderms. Illustrated. 32 pages. Paper. 30 cts.
- VI. Hyatt's Mollusca. Illustrated. 65 pages. Paper. 30 cts.
- VII. Hyatt's Worms and Crustacea. Illustrated. 68 pages. Paper. 30 cts.
- VIII. Hyatt's Insecta. Illustrated. 324 pages. Cloth. $1.25.
- XII. Crosby's Common Minerals and Rocks. Illustrated. 200 pages. Paper, 40 cts. Cloth, 60 cts.
- XIII. Richard's First Lessons in Minerals. 50 pages. Paper. 10 cts.
- XIV. Bowditch's Physiology. 58 pages. Paper. 20 cts.
- XV. Clapp's 36 Observation Lessons in Minerals. 80 pages. Paper. 30 cts.
- XVI. Phenix's Lessons in Chemistry. 20 cts.
- Pupils' Note-Book to accompany No. 15. 10 cts.

Rice's Science Teaching in the School. With a course of instruction in science for the lower grades. 46 pag s. Paper. 25 cts.

Ricks's Natural History Object Lessons. Supplies information on plants and their products, on animals and their uses, and gives specimen lessons. Fully illustrated 332 pages. $1.50.

Ricks's Object Lessons and How to Give them.
Volume I. Gives lessons for primary grades. 200 pages. 90 cts.
Volume II. Gives lessons for grammar and intermediate grades. 212 pages. 90 cts.

Shaler's First Book in Geology. For high school, or highest class in grammar school. 272 pages. Illustrated. $1.00.

Shaler's Teacher's Methods in Geology. An aid to the teacher of Geology. 74 pages. Paper. 25 cts.

Smith's Studies in Nature. A combination of natural history lessons and language work. 48 pages. Paper. 15 cts.

See also our list of books in Science.

D. C. HEATH & CO., Publishers, Boston, New York, Chicago

Science.

Ballard's World of Matter. A guide to mineralogy and chemistry. $1.00.

Benton's Guide to General Chemistry. A manual for the laboratory. 35 cts.

Boyer's Laboratory Manual in Biology. An elementary guide to the laboratory study of animals and plants. 80 cts.

Chute's Physical Laboratory Manual. A well-balanced course in laboratory physics, requiring inexpensive apparatus. Illustrated. 80 cts.

Chute's Practical Physics. For high schools and colleges. $1.12.

Clark's Methods in Microscopy. This book gives in detail descriptions of methods that will lead any careful worker to successful results in microscopic manipulation. $1.60.

Coit's Chemical Arithmetic. With a short system of analysis. 50 cts.

Colton's Physiology. Experimental and descriptive. For high schools and colleges. Illustrated. $1.12.

Colton's Physiology, Briefer Course. For earlier years in high schools. Illustrated. 00 cts.

Colton's Practical Zoology. Gives a clear idea of the subject as a whole by the careful study of a few typical animals. 80 cts.

Grabfield and Burns's Chemical Problems. For review and drill. Paper. 25 cts.

Hyatt's Insecta. Illustrated. $1.25.

Orndorff's Laboratory Manual. Contains directions for a course of experiments in Organic Chemistry, arranged to accompany Remsen's Chemistry. Boards. 35 cts.

Remsen's Organic Chemistry. An introduction to the study of the compounds of carbon. For students of the pure science, or its application to arts. $1.20.

Roberts's Stereo-Chemistry. Its development and present aspects. $1.00

Sanford's Experimental Psychology. Part I. Sensation and Perception. $1.50.

Shaler's First Book in Geology. For high school, or highest class in grammar school $1.00. Bound in boards for supplementary reader. 60 cts.

Shepard's Inorganic Chemistry. Descriptive and qualitative; experimental and inductive; leads the student to observe and think. For high schools and colleges. $1.12.

Shepard's Briefer Course in Chemistry, with chapter on Organic Chemistry. For schools giving a half year or less to the subject, and schools limited in laboratory facilities. 80 cts.

Shepard's Laboratory Note-Book. Blanks for experiments; tables for the reactions of metallic salts. Can be used with any chemistry. Boards. 35 cts.

Spalding's Introduction to Botany. Practical exercises in the study of plants by the laboratory method. 80 cts.

Stevens's Chemistry Note-Book. Laboratory sheets and cover, with separate cover for permanent file. 50 cts.

Venable's Short History of Chemistry. $1.00.

Whiting's Physical Measurement. I. Fifty measurements in Density, Heat, Light, and Sound. II. Fifty measurements in Sound, Dynamics, Magnetism, Electricity. III. Principles and Methods of Physical Measurement, Physical Laws and Principles, and Mathematical and Physical Tables. IV. Appendix. Parts I-IV, in one vol., $4.00.

Whiting's Mathematical and Physical Tables. Paper. 50 cts.

Williams's Modern Petrography. Paper. 25 cts.

For elementary works see our list of
books in Elementary Science.

D. C. HEATH & CO., Publishers, Boston, New York, Chicago.

THE HEART OF OAK BOOKS

A Series of Reading Books for Home and School; Edited
by Professor Charles Eliot Norton, of Harvard University

NOTE

By referring to the tables of contents the reader will discover that the Heart of Oak Books contain an unusual number of prose extracts of considerable length, to which justice cannot well be done in a small number of selections like this. Attention is called to some of the more noteworthy of these :

Book II. "Sindbad the Sailor" (56 pages). "The Death of Cæsar," from North's Plutarch (12 pages). "The Stories of Wallace and Bruce," from Scott's Tales of a Grandfather (77 pages).

Book III. "The Adventures of Ulysses," Charles Lamb (118 pages).

Book V. "Story of Argalus and Partheneia," Sir Philip Sidney (17 pages.) "Of Poets and Poetry," ibid. (11 pages). "Recollections of Christ's Hospital," Lamb (15 pages).

Book VI. Carlyle's "Boswell's Life of Johnson" (23 pages). Carlyle's "Burns" (22 pages), and "Scott" (27 pages). Hawthorne's "Custom House" from the Scarlet Letter (25 pages).

D. C. HEATH & CO., Publishers,

BOSTON   NEW YORK   CHICAGO

English Literature.

The Arden Shakespeare. The plays in their literary aspect, each with introduction, inter. pretative notes, glossary, and essay on metre. 40 cts.

Burke's American **Orations.** (A. J. GEORGE.) Five complete selections. 50 cts.

Burns's Select Poems. (A. J. GEORGE.) 118 poems chronologically arranged, with introduction, **notes** and glossary. Illustrated. 75 cts.

Coleridge's Principles **of Criticism.** (A. J. GEORGE.) From the *Biographia Literaria*. With portrait. 60 cts.

Cook's Judith. With introduction, translation, and glossary. Cloth. 170 pages **$1.00.** *Student's Edition*, without translation. Paper. 104 pages. 30 cts.

Cook's The Bible and **English Prose Style.** 40 cts.

Corson's Introduction to Browning. A guide to the study of Browning's **poetry.** Also has 33 poems with notes. With portrait of Browning. **$1.00.**

Corson's Introduction to the Study **of Shakespeare.** A critical study of Shakespeare's art, with comments on nine plays. **$1.00.**

Davidson's Prolegomena to Tennyson's In Memoriam. A critical analysis, with an index of the poem. 50 cts.

DeQuincey's Confessions of **an** Opium Eater. (G. A. WAUCHOPE.) A complete and scholarly edition. 50 cts.

Hall's Beowulf. A metrical translation. 75 cts. *Student's edition*, 30 cts.

Hawthorne and Lemmon's American **Literature.** Contains sketches, characterizations, and selections. Illustrated with **portraits.** $1.12.

Hodgkins's Nineteenth Century **Authors.** Gives full list of aids for library study of 26 authors. A separate pamphlet on **each** author. Price, 5 cts. each, or $3.00 per hundred. Complete in cloth. 60 cts.

Meiklejohn's History of English Language and Literature. For high schools and colleges. A compact and reliable statement of the essentials. 80 cts.

Moulton's Four Years of Novel-Reading. A reader's guide. 50 cts.

Moulton's Literary Study of the Bible. An account of the leading forms of literature represented, without reference to theological matters. **$2.00.**

Plumptre's Translation of Aeschylus. With biography and appendix. $1.00.

Plumptre's Translation of Sophocles. With biography and appendix. $1.00.

Shelley's Prometheus Unbound. (VIDA D. SCUDDER.) With introduction and notes 60 cts.

Simonds's Introduction to the Study of English Fiction. With illustrative selections. 80 cts. *Briefer Edition*, without illustrative selections. Boards. 30 cts.

Simonds's **Sir Thomas Wyatt and his Poems.** With biography, and critical analysis of his poems. 50 cts.

Webster's Speeches. (A. J. GEORGE.) Nine select speeches with notes. 75 cts.

Wordsworth's Prefaces and **Essays on Poetry.** (A. J. GEORGE.) Contains the best of Wordsworth's prose. 50 cts.

Wordsworth's Prelude. (A. J. GEORGE.) Annotated for high schools and colleges. Never before published alone. 75 cts.

Selections **from** Wordsworth. (A. J. GEORGE.) 168 poems chosen with a view to illustrate the growth of the poet's mind and art. 75 cts.

See also our list of books in Higher English and English Classics.

D. C. HEATH & CO., Publishers, Boston, New York, Chicago

MUSIC.

Whiting's Public School Music Course. Six books, forming a complete course for each class from primary to highest grammar grades. Books Nos. 1 to 5, Bds., each 30 cts. Book No. 6. Boards. 60 cts.

Whiting's Sixth Music Reader, *Girls' Edition.* Designed for use in the last two years of the grammar school, girls' high schools, young ladies' seminaries, and colleges. 60 cts.

Whiting's Part-Song and Chorus Book. For high and other schools. Vocal exercises; solfeggios; three- and four-part songs (for mixed and female voices); sacred choruses, etc. Boards. $1.10.

Whiting's Young Folk's Song-Book. A text-book for ungraded schools. Boards. 40 cts.

Whiting's Complete Music Reader. A complete course for high school, academies, etc. Boards. 85 cts.

Whiting's Music Charts. First Series, 30 charts, bound, $6.00. Second Series, 14 charts, bound, $3.00. (Easel for Music Charts, $1.50.)

Whittlesey and Jamieson's Harmony in Praise. A collection of Hymns with responsive Biblical selections, for college and school chapel exercises and for families. 85 cts.

Hart's School Manual of Classic Music. Contains portraits, sketches of the lives, and characteristic selections from the great masters. Boards. 212 pages. $1.15.

Pray's Motion Songs. Contains sixty pleasing songs, with gestures indicated. Boards. Illustrated. 45 cts.

Supplementary Music for Public Schools. Eight pp. numbers, 3 cts. Twelve pp. numbers, 4 cts. Sixteen pp. numbers, 5 cts. *Send for complete list.* New numbers are constantly being added.

Wilson's Infant School Drill. Exercises, with music, for the healthy development of the body. 32 pages. Square 8vo. Illustrated. Limp cloth. 25 cts.

Sent by mail, postpaid, on receipt of price.

D. C. HEATH & CO., PUBLISHERS,

BOSTON. NEW YORK. CHICAGO.

DRAWING AND MANUAL TRAINING.

Anthony's Mechanical Drawing. 98 pages of text, and 32 folding plates. $1.50.

Anthony's Machine Drawing. 50 pages of text, and 15 folding plates. $1.25.

Daniels' Freehand Lettering. 34 pages of text, and 13 folding plates. 85 cts.

Lunt's Brushwork for Kindergarten and Primary School. 18 lesson-cards in colors, with teacher's pamphlet, in envelope. 30 cts.

Johnson's Progressive Lessons in Needlework. Explains needlework from its rudiments and gives with illustrations full directions for work during six grades. 117 pages. Square 8vo. Cloth, $1.00. Boards, 60 cts.

Seidel's Industrial Instruction (Smith). A refutation of all objections raised against industrial instruction. 170 pages. 90 cts.

Thompson's Educational and Industrial Drawing.
Primary Free-Hand Series (Nos. 1–4). Each No., per doz., $1.00.
Primary Free-Hand Manual. 114 pages. Paper. 40 cts.
Advanced Free-Hand Series (Nos. 5–8). Each No., per doz., $1.50.
Model and Object Series (Nos. 1–3). Each No., per doz., $1.75.
Model and Object Manual. 84 pages. Paper. 35 cts.
Æsthetic Series (Nos. 1–6). Each No., per doz., $1.50.
Æsthetic Manual. 174 pages. Paper. 60 cts.
Mechanical Series (Nos. 1–6). Each No., per doz., $2.00.
Mechanical Manual. 172 pages. Paper. 75 cts.

Thompson's Manual Training, No. 1. Treats of Clay Modelling, Stick and Tablet Laying, Paper Folding and Cutting, Color, and Construction of Geometrical Solids. Illustrated. 66 pages. Large 8vo. Paper. 30 cts.

Thompson's Manual Training, No. 2. Treats of Mechanical Drawing, Clay-Modelling in Relief, Color, Wood Carving, Paper Cutting and Pasting. Illustrated. 70 pp. Large 8vo. Paper. 30 cts.

Waldo's Descriptive Geometry. A large number of problems systematically arranged, with suggestions. 85 pages. 90 cts.

Whitaker's How to Use Wood Working Tools. Lessons in the uses of the universal tools: the hammer, knife, plane, rule, chalk-line, square, gauge, chisel, saw, and auger. 104 pages. 60 cts.

Woodward's Manual Training School. Its aims, methods, and results; with detailed courses of instruction in shop-work. Fully illustrated. 374 pages. Octavo. $2.00.

Sent postpaid by mail on receipt of price.

D. C. HEATH & CO., PUBLISHERS,
BOSTON.   NEW YORK.   CHICAGO.

THE NATURAL SYSTEM OF

Vertical Writing

By A. F. NEWLANDS and R. K. ROW.   *Six Books.   Per doz., 75 cts.*

Some of the special merits of our system are : —

Practicability. It is the outgrowth of nearly five years' experience in vertical writing with thousands of pupils of all school ages. The authors of other series have not had this experience.

Strength. The books are in marked contrast to most of the systems recently published, which are efforts to adapt the sloping hand to the upright position.

Harmony. This system has been carefully worked out with a central idea as to form and movement.

Ease. Our round vertical script can be easily written. Engravers often produce graceful forms and combinations, but such as one cannot reproduce easily with the pen.   Every form and combination in our system has been thoroughly tested to avoid such difficulties.

Rapidity. Many of the letter-forms at first considered because they were artistic and graceful, after having been put to the test were discarded because they did not permit rapid execution.

Educative. The copies in the primary numbers are large and are illustrated with tasty outline drawings, stimulating interest in the writing and correlating reading, number, nature study, and spelling with the special writing lesson.   So far as practicable the correlation of studies has been carried throughout the series.   The size of the letter forms is gradually reduced in the first four numbers.

Economy. Such facilities have been secured for their manufacture, that books of the very best quality will be furnished at the very lowest prices.

Descriptive circular and sample copies sent on request.

D. C. HEATH & CO., Publishers

BOSTON   NEW YORK   CHICAGO   LONDON

www.ingramcontent.com/pod-product-compliance
Lightning Source LLC
Chambersburg PA
CBHW030127030726
47498CB00007B/2591